66 Oak Tree Dr.

Johnathan Sparks

Published by High Strangeness, 2020.

66 OAK TREE DR.

First edition. March 2, 2020.

Copyright © 2020 Johnathan Sparks.

ISBN: 978-1777142506

Written by Johnathan Sparks.

PART ONE

I give you this story as the only memory the universe may ever have of my existence. This is a true story, but you don't need to believe. You just need to listen – to allow a version of the truth to exist somewhere in your mind.

The name of my town will not be mentioned and every name in this story – including mine – has been altered. Everything but the address: 66 OakTree Dr.

• • • •

IT ALL STARTED WITH the note.

It was late October of 2009 in a small Ontario town. I had my first job working at a No Frills grocery store. After relying on my parents for so long, it was nice to have an income of my own. Averaging one hundred and twenty dollar paychecks seemed like a lot at seventeen. Stocking shelves was about as exciting as reading this sentence over and over, but I liked the people I worked with and it wasn't too physically demanding.

I first heard about the door during a closing shift with Mike Veller. I called him V. He had been filling the bread section beside the produce department. The store closed in about twenty minutes and I was done everything early. As I wandered, V called me over. He kept his head into his work, stuffing Wonder Bread deep into the shelves which hung below a dark window. His usual comedic attitude was gone and his voice kept at a volume which implied he had a secret.

V was twenty-two at the time. He didn't go to school, he drove a so-so car, and he lived with his parents. I think he had a couple of friends, people he talked to at work, but I sensed a loneliness about him. I didn't blame him. He was never around anyone his age, including girls. The girls at work were high school girls. Most of the part-time guys were, too. The full-timers were mainly all married with kids. V was stuck in the middle.

"Dan," he said as I approached. "Believe in ghosts?"

I nodded. I had never seen anything concrete, but I *had* seen the shadow of a man in my basement – my empty basement – and it so happened to be in the same year that the man who had built our home and lived in it for forty years had passed away in retirement living.

V breathed a sigh of relief, but stopped himself. "Good. None of my friends do," he stuffed the last loaf onto the shelf then turned to me, collapsing the blue tray the bread had come in. "There's something weird going on."

"What, here?" I looked around. The store was empty, minus a woman poking around in produce.

"Not in the store. North of town."

Nothing but forest, farms, and fields could be found north of my town. You could have the largest, loudest field party out there and the cops would almost never show.

"What do you mean?" I asked.

"Okay, look," he stared at the woman for a moment, assuring that she was out of earshot. "A few days ago I was texted an address. 66 OakTree Dr. For some reason, I couldn't find the number it was sent from. Just a name," he paused. "Kate. Curiosity got the best of me, so I got into my car and searched for the address. My GPS brought it up somewhere north of town. When I got close to the dot, my GPS froze and shut off," he sighed. "It's still broken. Because of this, I couldn't find the address and ended up getting lost. Then I came upon this road – a strange road which almost seemed to be a tunnel into the trees and bushes. It was unmaintained and kinda hilly. Some parts were muddy, some parts were filled with holes, but my car didn't have a problem," he looked around. "Then I saw it."

"Saw what?"

"The door."

"What? In the road?"

"Yeah. A real old fashioned one, you know, arched at the top and stuff," he cleared his throat. "Just as I was about to reverse out of the road – it was too small for a three-point – my headlights caught glimpse of it. Just... there, in a miniature clearing, pushed into the side of some sort of hill. But the hill looked cut in half or something, so dirt and roots surrounded it."

"Okay, what are you talking about?" I asked. This sounded silly, like he was reciting a dream.

But he ignored me, his eyes lost in the memory.

"A large oak tree shot out of this knoll. I think the tree is what the door was made out of. So, I got out of my car."

"What?" I said a little too loud. Despite having trouble suspending my disbelief, I thought that was crazy.

"Yeah," he nodded, his face stern. "I went over to the door and looked through the key hole, but couldn't see a thing. I grabbed the knob, but had to pull back. It was freezing cold – like painfully. So, I pulled down my sleeve and grabbed it again. It was locked."

"So, what'd you do?"

"I knocked."

"And?"

"This is the weirdest part," he glanced around some more. "Someone knocked back. It was a chilling knock. As though it weren't made from a fist, but..."

He looked at the ground. I wanted him to continue, but I also worried that I should leave it be. "Well," I patted his arm. "Just don't go back there."

"That's the thing," he said. "I got another text. From Kate."

"And?" I blurted.

"It told me to look in my desk drawer. I did. There was a key I'd never seen before. One of those really old ones that you'd see around Halloween."

I stared at him with wide eyes, unsure of if I believed him. "So, like, uh..." came out of my mouth.

"Come with me," he said.

"Oh no," I shook my head.

"I don't want to go alone."

"I don't want to find a phantom door *or* see what lies on the other side. Are you sure you weren't drunk or something?"

He sighed. "Never mind."

I felt bad. I thought about it that entire night after work. And at school the next day. Perhaps I *would* go with him. It was probably just a natural art piece someone had made in the middle of the woods for fun. And maybe someone was already there and wanted to scare him. I decided to go to the store after school and let V know that I had changed my mind.

. . . .

I WALKED THROUGH THE parking lot quickly, the October wind chilling my summer hangover. I looked over at his car to make sure he wasn't on break and *hacking a dart* as he'd like to say. He wasn't. I walked through the doors and went up to another one of my co-workers who had already graduated high school. He was cutting open cases of Ragu and sliding them onto the shelf.

"Hey, where's V?" I asked.

He turned to me. "I have no idea, man. Have you heard from him?"

"No," I started to walk off. "Is he in his office or something?"

He didn't actually have an office. The running joke was that the bathroom stalls were our offices, the toilet paper our important files. The toilet itself would be your computer so you could say you were in the office sitting on the computer.

"No," the tone of his voice stopped me. "No one has seen him all day. He didn't show up for work. We called his mom, but she hasn't seen him since he left for work yesterday."

"Okay, thanks," I tried to brush it off as nothing as I rushed around the corner. Because it likely was nothing. He probably went to a friend's house, forgot he worked, and his cell phone died.

I walked out of the store. The October wind didn't chill me anymore. V's car did. Why was it there if he wasn't? I turned to the north. I couldn't see very far, but I looked anyway. My mind jumped to conclusions. Somewhere out there, V found something. He tried to ask for my help and now he's gone.

• • • •

I DON'T THINK V SUBSCRIBED to long-term goals. It would explain his situation. Maybe he found them daunting or pointless – favouring short-term pleasures over delayed gratification. Whatever the case, I believe he felt like he was trapped in his job and town. I also think I was the person in the store who knew him best. We didn't talk *that* much, but when we did we got on really well together. This is why his car haunted me after he disappeared. It had been sitting in the parking lot for months. The snow built up on it with each fall, then dissipated throughout the week. It would watch me every time I walked through the parking lot. But one Saturday morning – the first Saturday of 2010, and the morning I found the note – the spectating was especially present.

There was a Tim Horton's outside of the store, connected to a plaza. All you had to do was cross the parking lot and there you were with the donuts and hot beverages. I took my first break at 10 a.m., heading over to Timmies to get myself a donut and a hot chocolate. It was a bright, cold day. Freezing, actually. The kind of day where the frigidness enters your lungs and burrows into the deepest parts of your body with no remorse. Hence, the hot chocolate.

I felt the presence more than ever when I stepped out of the store, the automatic doors knocking shut behind me. I shoved my hands in my pocket as I waited for a car to pass by. Its tires crunched the frozen snow beneath like it was Styrofoam.

I always wanted to look anywhere other than V's car, but my eyes landed on it every time. I didn't understand why it hadn't been towed. But of course, I wasn't going to be the one to say anything.

The sun's reflection on whatever snow it could find burned my eyes. When the pain faded, I saw something different about his red Cavalier in the far end of the parking lot. A note stuck from beneath the windshield wiper, waving in the wind. My mind protested going to look, but curiosity shoved it out.

I approached the car, expecting to find a desperate letter from a distraught family member. I stood beside the driver's side fender and peered at the slip of paper. The wiper blade concealed a scribbled message in red. I didn't want to remove my hands from the warmth of my pockets, but I did. I lifted the wiper – a line of recently broken ice under it – and pulled out the note. What it said burned a sensation inside of me, sparking a sweat even in the winter's breeze.

My mind went back to that night. The night I had finished early and wandered my department. The night I was told something I laughed off as nothing.

The night V went missing.

PART TWO

When I got into my bedroom after work, I sat at my computer and stuck my hand into my pocket for the note. I hoped that it somehow wouldn't be there. That maybe it disappeared and the whole scene was nothing but a cold winter fancy. But instead, it fell out of my hand and onto my desk, the messily written words facing me.

66 OakTree Dr.
– V

I Googled it and found a few things. An address in Levittown, Pennsylvania. Another somewhere in Australia. One in the United Kingdom. So, I added *Ontario* to the search. Nothing coherent showed up.

I recalled V telling me that he punched it into his GPS and received a location north of town. I ran downstairs for the gadget and brought it back into my room. When I punched it in, the only result was a 66 Oak Tree Crt in Wasaga Beach. That was north of Toronto and a three-hour drive from my town. There was no way that was it.

I dropped it onto my desk and stared blankly into my computer screen. There were a lot of unmaintained roads north of my town and I had no idea where to start. But I had to try. I pulled out my phone and texted my friend.

Dan> *Hey Allyster. What are you doing tonight?*

He promptly replied.

Allyster> Not much, man... wanna come over?

Dan> I'll stop by around 8.

Allyster> Kk see you then.

Anxiety waved through me. The gears were spinning and they would turn me to the door. What if I found it? What if V was there, dead? The thought petrified me. And it sent another thought through my mind. I knew about the door, but didn't tell anyone. Not his mother, not the police. If I did find him, I'd have some explaining to do. I had to either get a story together, or keep it all to myself.

• • • •

ALLYSTER LIVED IN A six-plex on a quiet street off of my town's downtown strip. This was almost on the other side of town from my house, so it sent me walking through random streets. On a typical summer night, you might find a small number of people walking down these streets, hear noises from backyards, or see people out on their porches. But on the winter nights, you went a long while before seeing another person. In a few houses per street – behind lawns of frozen snow – ghostly curtains hung, illuminated by a light from within. The remaining houses stood hard and dark, defeated by the cold.

On my walks to Allyster's, my feet usually crunched the snow that the plow failed to collect. But no snow remained that night, so my feet quietly patted along the salt-stained road. Apart from the odd car passing through or the painful whine of a loose serpentine belt on a car a few streets over, I was a lone survivor, moving through a desolate town like a character from *The Stand*. Oftentimes, I *did* like to pretend I was the last person on earth, wandering the streets. But a car or someone stepping down from their apartment for a smoke would ruin the fantasy.

Though, that night I couldn't pretend at all. It felt as though someone *was* with me, following me. But I found the streets barren – just snowbanks and low temperatures – each time I turned around to look.

Allyster's apartment was about a half hour walk from my house. Though, I've been known to do it in twenty minutes if the cold pushed me fast enough. And this night was one of those nights.

I entered the small foyer of his building and pulled my hands out of my jean pockets – a futile attempt to shield them from the cold. With frozen fingers which typed in slow-mo, I sent him a text to come down and let me inside. After a few seconds of silence, I heard a click from upstairs and the thuds of him coming around the corners.

Allyster was athletic. He went running almost daily and played on the school's football team. Though I didn't pay attention to sports, I heard he was one of their best players. He probably could have thrived at other sports had he not gotten the short stick of his parent's divorce. He lived with his dad in the apartment, and his mom had remarried and moved to British Columbia. His dad seemed to be in and out of jobs, never at home, but since Allyster's mom had married wealthy, she would routinely send him money. Though, not enough to be an active participant in organized sports. Not to mention away games, to which he'd never have a ride.

He came down the stairs, shirtless, in the midst of texting someone. He was probably home alone, working out with a movie on. Allyster thing to do. I just hoped that he was in a serious mood, or could at least muster one up.

"Sup, man?" he said as he opened the door and turned back up the stairs.

I followed him up, excited for warmth. His apartment was small, but cozy. I don't mean that in a polite way. It really was cozy. He had a couch made for kings and no matter how cold it got outside, the place remained toasty. I enjoyed looking out of his living room's bay window at a snow storm, standing in my t-shirt sans a chill. It gave me the satisfaction that we'd had the elements beat.

"I've still got some of that cake you brought over last time," he said as we got inside. "Want a slice?"

"Sure," I sat down on his couch. *Stranger Than Fiction*, the Will Ferrell movie, played on his TV. I pulled out my phone, swiping through the apps, trying to seem busy while I gathered my thoughts. I had to tell him about the door without mentioning V.

He dropped a plate of chocolate cake on the coffee table before me. He then plopped down on the other side of the sofa and gouged the slab which sat on his own plate.

"So," I switched my phone for the cake and leaned back onto the couch. "What were you gonna do tonight?"

"Nothing, man," he said with half a fork load still in his mouth. "I was here watching a movie when Lauren texted me. I ignored it," he said quickly with raised eyebrows, as if to assure me. "It's been almost a month since we broke up and she still randomly texts me. Like, that's what happens when you cheat on someone – they dump you and don't want to talk anymore. I just wished she'd get the hint."

"Well..." I started, but he cut me off.

"She just gets me thinking, you know. So, I started working out. I need to not think about her." Another load of cake went into his mouth.

This was perfect. I felt bad for him, but he was in a serious mood and needed something to keep him busy. I think I had what he needed. But I had to play it easy. I had to start with some advice.

I wasn't quite a lady's man. I had a tough time with girls. They always liked me, but not like *that*. They wanted to be my best friend for life. Don't get me wrong, I didn't get friend-zoned by *all* girls. Just the girls I liked. Looking back, I think I purposefully crushed on girls I knew I couldn't get. Feeling bad for myself was a hobby of mine. And also let me say, I really liked my friends that were girls. I felt more comfortable with them. Once my stupid, hopeless-romantic brain accepted the fact that they didn't want to marry me someday, I realized how much easier it could be to talk to girls.

Sorry for the digression, but understand that it's hard not to analyze as I recount the events which led up to my encounter. And the subsequent events which resulted in my current predicament.

At any rate, I believed that – despite my lack of experience – I could deliver some sound advice when it came to relationships. Especially if it meant finding V.

"I don't think any girl who treats you like that deserves any part of your mind," I said after swallowing some cake. "Seriously, you should just tell her you've moved on."

"Yeah," he twisted his face. "I just don't know, man. Like, a part of me still wants her."

I shook my head. "Look, it's entirely up to you, but once a cheater always a cheater – I mean it. After they get away with it once, they think 'oh, things are back to normal and going well now, I could always recuperate if I did it again,'" I sighed. "I just think it's a bad idea. I also think that someone better will come along. Trust me. You've got to be you and do what you love and she'll come to you."

He nodded while chewing an ungodly amount of cake, patting me on the shoulder. "You're so right, man."

"Good," I said. "And I know what we can do tonight to keep your mind off of it."

"What's that?"

"North of town there's a door."

He stared at me. The same stare I gave V a few months ago.

"Like, in a house?"

"No, just... in the woods. Like, it's in a hill."

"Where does it lead to?"

"Nobody knows. A few of the guys from work were talking about it. I think we should go find it."

"Okay," he said, seeming a bit excited. "Where is it?"

"I don't know."

I wanted to tell him about the note and the address on it – something that would peak his interest monstrously – but it would also lead back to V. In retrospect, telling Allyster the whole truth in this moment would have led things down a better road – a road with two determined people instead of one determined person and one mildly interested person.

"Okay," he slowly nodded. "How do we get north of town?"

A brick hit my chest. How could I be so stupid that I didn't even think of that? The northern outskirts were an easy forty-minute walk from Allyster's building. And biking in this cold would be as stupid as stealing a car.

"Frig, I don't know," I mumbled.

But then the answer came. It came in the form of my phone vibrating on the table. It came just when we needed it, and after the way everything played out, I know that it was no coincidence.

I picked up my phone and read the message.

2895551028> *Hey, it's Melissa. What's up?*

Obviously this didn't mean much yet, but it would in a minute – after I added her name into my phone and found out why a girl like Melissa had decided to text me.

Melissa was a year older than Allyster and me. I met her through a play we were both cast in for school. It wasn't high budget or anything, but we all had fun together. Melissa and her friend Hannah were in it, but at first we didn't speak much. See, Melissa was a singer, a dancer, a high honours student, and her last boyfriend was the hottest guy in the school. Don't get me wrong, I *wanted* to talk to her. Quite a bit, actually. And luckily, my friend, Eric, who was cast as second lead, knew Hannah. That small connection led to us all occupying the same table during rehearsal breaks. Eventually it developed into the odd hang-out at lunch and some group chatting over Facebook.

Needless to say, if I had been standing, I would have fallen over upon seeing a text from her on my phone. And I had yet to even take into consideration that she had her driver's licence.

I didn't tell Allyster. I just quietly replied. I knew he needed an emotional rebound, especially after what I had said, and I didn't want that to cripple my chances of whatever could be happening here. Allyster was athletic and muscular. I was skinny and never cared so much about how my hair looked before leaving the house. Okay, I could fix my hair, but who has the time? The point is, Allyster didn't require my help when it came to finding a girlfriend. I, on the other hand, did, and optimistic me saw this as something.

Dan> *Nothing. Just with my friend, Allyster.*

My phone vibrated before I could put it back down. I looked up to see that Allyster had started watching the movie. So, I went back into my phone without a worry.

Melissa> *Is that the quarterback for our school? And just driving around with Hannah. We can pick you guys up if you're bored?*

I ignored the first question. My chances had already started to leak and all I did was give a name. Still, seventeen-year-old me was ecstatic. Though, deep down, I wondered if she would have sent that invite if Allyster wasn't with me. If that were the case, when it came to looking for V, I should have been grateful for his presence.

"Dude," I said. "I know how we can look for it."

He shifted his attention from the TV to me.

"You know that Melissa girl from the play?"

He nodded.

"Her and her friend Hannah want to go for a drive. We can get them to come look with us."

"Sweet!" His eyes lit up. He was thinking what I was thinking. This wasn't good news. I prepared to pour my chances down the drain. Maybe it was for the best. Why get all worked up anyhow? Like Weezer said, *Why Bother?* I needed to stay focused on finding the door. On finding V and figuring out what went wrong – finding out who, if anyone, took him, and why he disappeared without his car.

I texted her Allyster's address and told her we'd wait outside.

PART THREE

Ten minutes later we were in the backseat of Melissa's parent's Volvo and I had already explained the censored version of the door to her and Hannah.

"It's an unmaintained road, apparently," I said.

Their interest flourished. This was good news. We headed north, toward the door – the last thing V might have ever seen. Though the sternness of the situation was only recognized by me, I didn't want to kill my first impression by obsessing. I had to be grateful that we had the opportunity to search for the door. Not to mention the chance to make new friends.

Hannah had brown hair to match her eyes and freckles, and Melissa was a redhead with a big smile. Hannah sat in the passenger seat, Allyster sat behind her, and I behind Melissa. She glanced in the rear-view mirror frequently. At the time, I thought – and so frantically hoped – that she kept looking at *me*. But now I understand that she was merely being a cautious driver.

They talked about how Allyster played on the football team and how great that was. It pitted something foul in my chest as they both awed at it. I didn't really have anything awe-worthy. I could've told them about my level 80 Paladin in World of Warcraft, but for some reason I didn't think they'd flatter me for it. Warcraft simply kept me company on late nights and snow days. And the first rule of Warcraft was that you don't talk about Warcraft in real life. It existed as a place where people could go and be great in other ways. The game was an escape.

I kept my gaze out the car window as they talked about a few others on the football team. We passed the Tim Horton's by No Frills and carried on north. A few car dealerships came and went and the falling number of houses signaled that we would soon be with the trees.

I put my attention back into the car. Amidst my thoughts, I hadn't noticed the silence. As it grew awkward, I prepared to pull out my phone – my awkward situation defense system. Before I could, I caught a glimpse of Melissa glancing at me through the mirror with a smile. She clicked the radio on to a pop song. I didn't know the song, but Melissa's and Hannah's enthusiasm made what came through the speakers seem exciting. They sang and moved with the music, insisting between lines that Allyster and I join them.

We looked at each other with a laugh. We didn't know the words, but we moved to the music anyway. It didn't take long for me to forget how un-awe-worthy I thought I was.

We listened to more music and chatted. We talked about the play and how nervous we were for opening night. They told anecdotes about each other, some that weren't funny, but their zest and laughter somehow made them funny. Allyster and I told some of our funny stories – things of the past that had made us laugh.

"Eric, Allyster, and I were at Tim Horton's," I giggled, being at a point where everything seemed funny. "We sat down with our stuff while Allyster ordered. When he got back to the table, he said, 'I thought we were going back to my place?' Eric replied right away, 'I thought *you* were going back to your place and we were staying here?'"

We busted up with laughter.

"Allyster was so pissed, we had to follow him back to his place the whole way because he didn't want to walk with us."

As we settled our laughs, I took a look out the window. We were passing the Tim Horton's again. We had been driving for hours, just talking.

"We forgot about the door," I said.

"Oh yeah," Melissa replied. "I'm sorry, guys."

"Me too," Hannah said. "How about tomorrow night? We will look for real."

"Deal."

• • • •

THE NEXT NIGHT WAS a Sunday night, but we had Monday off, as it was the last day of Christmas holidays. We drove around the northern woods aimlessly, going down every unmaintained road we knew of, but we couldn't find anything that resembled a door. The interest waned in the group, and – following road after road of dead or snow covered foliage – the fantastical idea of this strange door in the woods seemed too imaginary to be real. If only V had told me which street it stemmed off of.

I worried everyone thought the whole thing was a joke. I wanted to tell them not to tell anyone, but I thought that that'd come off as odd. I couldn't risk anything that could lead back to V.

So, I decided to pretend I didn't care either and let the thing fall away from their minds.

• • • •

ON THE TUESDAY MORNING I awoke to a blizzard. I checked Facebook and saw statuses everywhere acknowledging that it was a snow day. An extra day off of school never hurt anyone.

I did what I did every snow day and loaded Warcraft while heading to the kitchen for some cereal. My parents weren't home and my sister was still asleep. But even with the perfect atmosphere, I couldn't get into the game. There would be no escaping that morning. For the door haunted me. Despite deciding to forget about it, something pulled my mind to this place I couldn't find. I looked out the window at the whiteness on the ground, and the whiteness continuing to pile onto it all, and I thought about how much more difficult it'd now be to find the door.

That's when my phone vibrated, taking me out of the game even more so. It was Melissa.

Melissa> *Let's hang out tomorrow. After rehearsal.*

A one-on-one hangout. I stared at the screen as anxiety and excitement battled inside of me. If her and I had any potential of becoming more than friends, this was my chance.

But a following text killed the thought.

Melissa> *You, me, Allyster, and Hannah.*

Maybe she intended for a one-on-one hangout, but then backed out and sent the second text. I liked that idea better. Either way, I got to hang out with her. But if she was able to tell Allyster, that must've meant she was texting him, too.

I told myself to forget about it and that my expectations needed to be re-assessed.

And that I need to focus on the door. On V.

There was nothing I could do on such an inhibiting day, so I tried Google. I searched for *phantom doors, haunted doors,* and *doors in the woods,* but none of the results were relevant unless I wanted to build a wooden door or install a secret one in my bedroom.

For now, V would have to wait.

• • • •

I SPENT REHEARSAL EXCITED for what was next, my good mood tangible. Allyster sat in one of the audience seats, watching, waving at Melissa whenever she appeared on stage. When we got into her car at around 8 p.m., the sun was long gone. We sat in the same seats as the previous nights and hit the Timmies drive-thru for something warm.

"We know where to go," Melissa said as we left the Tim Horton's parking lot.

We drove west of town for a few minutes. Woodland and farms surrounded our town in all directions except one. We moved down a street occupied by rich homes. Some hid behind trees, while others revealed their size and glamour from the road.

We parked on the side of the country road, as far into the ditch as we could with all the snow.

"Come on," Melissa and Hannah giggled as we followed them across the road.

We walked in the dark, watching out for ice along a winding driveway. When it opened up to a property, we found construction vehicles and the silhouette of a house under the winter's moon. As we approached, it became clear that it was merely a shell. A type of plywood covered the exterior, hiding everything but the holes which would soon become the doors and windows. Inside there were support beams and the frames which would be strung with wires, filled with insulation, then finally covered forever by drywall.

Creeping through, I thought about the future residents of this home. Would they ever know that some kids were here, sneaking around for a laugh?

We went up the stairs, all the way up to the third floor. There were various points where one could fall right back down to the first floor – or even the basement – so we took our time, using our phones for lights when necessary. Allyster played the caring, overprotective boy role with Melissa and Hannah. The façade bugged me, but I was happy to see that Melissa wasn't buying into it much.

After messing around a bit, watching Allyster climb onto the roof for a minute, then scaring Hannah pretty good, I found myself isolated from the others. I could still hear their obscured voices, but couldn't see them. I wandered about on my own, thinking again of the home's future inhabitants. Then I heard something in a nearby room. At first it sounded like a shuffle – as though someone was dragging their feet upon the sawdust covered floor. But then it turned into a furious and quick scratching. I was timid, but wanted to investigate. I figured that a raccoon or a squirrel had briefly come out of hibernation – probably thanks to us – and I knew that so long as I didn't corner it, I should be fine.

I walked slowly toward the room which contained the noise, peering past the vertical two-by-fours which made up the frame. I saw only blackness. The moon wasn't reaching this side of the house.

I moved through the doorway and the scratching – almost right in front of me – grew frantic. I pulled out my phone and went to the flashlight app. As soon as the light filled the room, the noise stopped with a thud. Shining upon one of the outer walls, my phone's light revealed a horrid scene. A screwdriver lay on the floor. On the wall above it, words had been carved into the lumber:

Dan, please hel

Without a move, I looked around the empty room.

"Mike?" I breathed.

Nothing.

As I stood, unable to move, an overwhelming sense of terror pulsed through me with every beat of my heart. I knew I had to do something. I also had to confide in someone. And I knew exactly who that would be. Someone I wanted to get closer to. But she had to take it seriously. And for that to happen,

I had to tell it all to her. I had to show her the proof. I snapped a picture of the wall and went back with the group. Thankfully, we went home right after.

I texted Melissa when I got into bed.

> **Dan** > *On Saturday can we meet at Tim Horton's? 2pm? There's something I want to talk to you about.*

> **Melissa** > *Sure, see you then.*

PART FOUR

I carried two hot chocolates to a table and peeled off the lids. The steam poured out like it had been caged forever. It's smell – a smell of winter – calmed me. My heart had been racing and the reason seemed so stupid. But she could walk in at any second.

I looked out the Tim Horton's window, across the No Frills parking lot, and at V's car. I sat where I did on purpose. I wanted to be able to show her. That should be enough evidence for her to know I was telling the truth. I could show her the note, the picture, and the car. Then she would realize why I wanted to find the door. Fun was not my objective.

Panic rushed me when her car pulled in. It felt like I had waited a year – which would still be too little time to prepare – but the hot chocolate's warm steam told me otherwise. I started to sweat as I put the lids back on. I didn't want to smell. Not now. I zipped up my jacket as I watched her get out of the car. This was going to be the first time it was just me and her.

She stepped in and walked toward the table, her eyes scanning the restaurant. Red hair waved out of a black winter hat, ending mid-chest over a white jacket. For some reason she looked much more attractive than usual. This only accelerated my nerves.

"Hi, Dan," she said as she sat down, looking at the hot chocolate.

"Hey, Melissa," I pointed to the cup with the letters 'HC' marked on the lid. "I got that for you."

"Oh, thanks. But I don't really like hot chocolate."

"Is there anything else you want?" I glanced over at the menu. My mind raced for any excuse to delay the real reason I wanted to talk to her.

"No, thanks."

Her usual happy-go-lucky mood was gone. The tone of her voice suggested I had imposed on her Saturday. She removed her hat, and I sipped my hot chocolate. It scorched my tongue, but I pretended it didn't. I was clearly annoying her enough. And now I couldn't even think of what I wanted to say. Or how to bring it up.

"So," she broke the silence, her eyes scanning the restaurant again before locking with mine. "What did you want to talk to me about?"

I glanced out at V's car. I could barely see it. Another car had parked beside it, obstructing the view. This wasn't going as planned. I tried to think of something else I could tell her. I thought about the way she made me feel. How being with her made me feel. I only needed one sense. To see her, or smell her, or hear her voice and an eruption of butterflies would flow into my stomach.

But this time I was nervous. The two sensations produced an intense storm within my chest. Maybe I would tell her how I felt. It'd be best to let her know as soon as I did instead of waiting and being too late. I was sick of not telling girls how I felt, only to end up watching them find other guys.

"I, um," the words started to leave my mouth. "I've had fun the last few nights that, you know, we've all been hanging out."

"Me too," she said.

The tone of her response sent the feeling that she knew what was coming and didn't want to hear it. But I had to say it now. It was either confess my feelings, or announce that something supernatural has reached out to me. I feared bringing the latter to the table when she was acting so off. It was probably a stupid idea anyway.

"Well, I just wanted you to know..."

"What is it?" she tilted her head, staring at me like she cared. Maybe she *did* want me to say it.

"I, well, I like you."

"I like you, too," she said.

But I wasn't sold. That would have been too easy. I stared into her eyes. There was a tension there, like she had just made a mistake.

"Like, as friends," she added.

"Yeah, okay, sure," I nodded, stupidly sipping my lava hot beverage and giving myself another burn.

"Wait, did you mean, like...?"

I shrugged.

"Dan, I just..."

"It's okay," I said. "Really."

I gave her a fake smile. I tried to not let it weigh me down, but I was hurt – burnt like my tongue from the hot chocolate.

I looked away for a moment and saw something which spilled horror all over me. Allyster scurried through the parking lot. He was dressed better than me, but that was the usual. Even though my family was better off than his, it always appeared as though the opposite were true. He wore perfectly fitted jeans topped with a thick sweater which looked cozy – grandma knitted cozy. Even his boots knocked my worn Nikes out of the park. They clunked against the ground as he walked in. He glanced over and saw us, acting like we had a million dollars on the table for him.

"Hey guys!" he held up his hand. I gave him a high five, not wanting to act sour in front of Melissa. After my greeting, he turned to her with a smile. "Hey, Melissa, how's it going?"

"Good," she smiled for the first time since she had come in. It wasn't a dreamy smile in any way, more of a polite smile mixed with a legitimate one. Perhaps she wanted to mask it because I was there. Who knew now? I just shoveled dirt onto whatever friendship or relationship her and I could have possibly had.

"What're you guys doing?" he asked with enthusiasm.

But I could read him. Jealousy filled his veins.

"Oh, we were just getting some hot chocolate," she looked down at hers. "But I don't want mine. Do you?"

"Aw, thanks," he tilted his head, picking up the cup. "Can't survive this cold without some Timmies."

I faked a laugh. He was one of my best friends, but at that moment I just wanted him to leave. I was busy making a fool of myself.

"So, Melissa?" he stepped closer to her, making room for a passerby. "Are we still going to go tonight? You know, to look for the door?" He made a face which mocked fear.

"Yeah," she replied, giving me a quick glance. "Not that we will have any luck finding it."

Allyster also glanced at me like he realized he should have kept quiet. "Oh, hey, Dan, do you wanna come?"

"Nah, I'm busy."

I worried that he might pry, but he took it. He looked back down at Melissa and then at me with a joyful exhale and toothless smile. He held the hot chocolate closer to his face and smelt it.

"Well," he said. "I got what I came for. My dad is in No Frills, so I should probably go."

"I should go, too," Melissa put her hat back on and stood up. "Bye Dan," she looked at me.

Her eyes locked with mine for a moment. There was something in there. I didn't know if it was asking or telling. But they said more than just goodbye.

"See yah," I ignored it. "See yah, man," I waved to Allyster as they both headed out the doors.

They walked to her car where they stopped to chat. I prayed she wasn't telling him what I had said. Humiliation filled my chest as I slouched in my chair, fearing the worst. I glanced over at the neighbouring table to an old man with a newspaper laid out in front of him. He glanced up and gave me a *been there, son* look before focusing back down at the daily. I turned away too. My hot chocolate was finally at a good temperature, so I took a real sip and watched Allyster and Melissa say goodbye out in the cold. She got in her car and drove off as he ran back toward the store.

I stared at the car blocking V's. He vanished because of something to do with the door and now people were making it out to be another small town legend. But I knew that much more lurked about. I just didn't know what that *more* could be.

The car pulled away and revealed V's Cavalier. Why was his car parked there? Where is the door? And what's even behind it? Amidst the storm of questions, it came to me. If I wanted answers, I'd have to go looking for them.

Look in your desk drawer.

And I could only think of one place to find some clues.

V's bedroom.

PART FIVE

The night was frigid. It had to be the apex of our Canadian winter. But in mid-January, I knew that we were still in for the long haul.

A few days after my meeting with Melissa, I crept through my house in the middle of the night. I had bundled myself to the brim – half for warmth, half for the protection of my identity. Getting caught sneaking into V's house would set off an alarm too big for me to combat with some rambles of the paranormal. So, I had a hat, a neck gaiter, shoes I never wore, and a pair of thin gloves for warmth, but also precision. I could rob a bank on the way home if I wanted.

I quietly opened the back door and slipped outside. As my foot crunched the ice which covered the deck, I debated returning to my warm bed. But I couldn't. Not after what had happened in the half-built house.

V was waiting.

The moon shone bright, its light bouncing off of the snow-covered lawns. From up there it watched me pace down the road. And again, as I walked through the dead street, I didn't feel alone. Someone followed, cheering me on. Maybe it *was* the moon. For there was no one else to cheer me on in this quest of solitude. I had come to terms with my mistake of telling Allyster the half-truth about the door. Allyster was a good guy, and had I told him everything, I know he would have had my back one-hundred percent. But now talk of this phantom door circled my school and no one knew that it had to do with a story the local news had grown jaded of: a missing twenty-two-year-old.

I had first heard something about the door while waiting for the teacher in physics class. The talk didn't come from Allyster, who sat across the room, but from Brad Shostak and Greg McKinley. The two sat behind me, and when I'd heard the words *'the door'*, my ears perked. Brad had asked Greg if he'd heard about the ghost door and that his girlfriend, Taylor, had told him about it. Greg retorted that ghosts don't exist, and that the door was obviously where the leprechauns lived. I put my head down, guilt washing over me, knowing that I had to find V as soon as possible, whether or not that meant finding the door as well.

That's when Mr. Crowley walked in. His eyes – which seemed to spike out at you, grab you, and make you learn to like the lesson – did a quick scan of the classroom. He popped his suitcase onto the front table, ran a hand over his bald head, then took off his jacket.

"Mr. Crowley," Brad called from behind me. "Can doors to other dimensions exist in the woods?"

Amidst a few chuckles, the teacher looked past me to Brad like the boy had gone mad. "Don't be ridiculous," he replied. "Such a thing – if even possible – would require such a tremendous amount of energy that everyone from here to Calgary would know about it."

"See," Brad whispered to Greg. "Ghosts, not leprechauns."

I glanced over at Allyster, made eye contact with him, then quickly broke it. But in my peripherals, I saw him raise his hand. Mr. Crowley lifted the eyebrows which usually crushed his eyes and pointed to Allyster.

"What if the door didn't lead to another dimension?" he asked. "But, like, an extension of our own world?"

"I don't follow," Crowley replied.

"So, not a door to another world," Allyster paused. "But a door to a part of our world which we can't get to."

"Allyster," Crowley sighed. "That *would* be another dimension. See, the definition of dimension is flexible in physics. There are the dimensions in which we live. Time is somewhat considered a dimension. So, what you're asking is very complex. Let me just say this," he paused. "Since the energy required to open a portal would be so exotic, if there *were* a portal to another dimension, and if it were attached to no glaringly obvious apparatus, then consider the portal's origin to be not from our physical realm. In other words," he said. "It would have to have been opened from the other side."

• • • •

V LIVED A FEW STREETS away from mine. As far as I knew, it would only be his parents asleep in the red bungalow. I prayed that there were no guests there, aiding them during the hunt for their lost son. Little did they know, the person most likely to return V was about to break into their home.

I slowed down as I approached. There had been an adrenaline in me as I walked over, but it had since dissipated. The reality of it had hit me. How was I even going to get in? Was I really just going to break into someone's home?

The house came into view and my walk grew sluggish. Though I knew I couldn't stop. It would be too suspicious had anyone been watching. I needed to decide right then. I either continued walking and aborted the plan, or I walked up his driveway and into the backyard with confidence. If I acted like I belonged, no midnight observer could suspect a thing.

Without even a deep breath, I curved my walk toward his driveway. It was as though an exterior force engaged my body and took control, bringing me closer to his house. I knew I had to do it and appreciated the unknown boost of confidence.

A few moments and pounds of the heart later, I found myself at his back entrance. First, I was going to try the door. If locked, I'd have to settle on crawling through a window. I grabbed the handle and took a deep breath. It felt cold, even through my gloves. The knob on the other side – in V's dark house, where I needed to be – was most certainly warm. But either way, it wouldn't twist. The door was locked.

I stood in front of it, my hand still on the knob, warming it up. I wasn't sure if I was relieved or not. My chances of getting in through a window were slim, so the locked door marked the end of the night for me. If there were any secrets to be found, they weren't going to be found by me.

I wracked my brain, wondering where else I could go to find some clues. V's car sat in the No Frills parking lot, but it also sat in view of a security camera. And the night crew might catch me during their smoke breaks. It was too much risk for a possible dead-end.

A sound from behind – in the backyard – launched my heart into my throat. I spun around to an empty yard. My eyes scanned it viciously, trying to pinpoint the source of the sound. Any sane rodent would be well into hibernation.

I looked to the garden. Snow covered it, and a short fence about a foot high surrounded it. But one part of the garden wasn't concealed by snow. I stepped down from the doorstep, trying to utilize the moon's light. As I neared, it became clear that a rock the size of a small dinner plate had flipped over and hit the tiny fence. Beneath it lay a key.

Before I could freak out, a reassurance came over me – one, in retrospect, that I cannot explain. But something told me that I was doing a good thing. That my plan had purpose.

I grabbed the key and returned to the door. I slid it in, enjoying the tiny sound of the tumblers as they clicked into place. I then pulled open the door and slipped inside.

After taking an enormous amount of time to close the door sans a sound, I found myself on a small landing. A short staircase in front of me led up to the main floor, and stairs to the right descended into darkness. If I were a smart guy, I would have peeked through the windows first to find V's room. But since I had already made that oversight, I had to play the cards in my hand.

I figured I wanted to avoid the upstairs at all costs, for that would most likely be where his parents slept. So, I wagered and checked the basement first. I used the light from my phone's screen to guide me. I inched down the stairs and beyond them, being careful to not bump anything. I had the entire night to be stealthy.

To my right came a doorway without a door. Before I could venture inside, my phone's glow revealed that boxes and other junk filled it. I continued, checking the side to the left of the staircase. It was much more open. I moved into it, slowly, like the grandfather clock which ticked somewhere within the dark basement. Eventually, my light revealed an entertainment room. A TV, couch, chairs, the whole shebang. I left it behind with the stairs and the storage room and carried on deeper into the basement.

A few more blind steps and I came to an ajar door. I stood for a moment, recalling the stairway's distance in case I had to bolt back up it and into the cold. Then, with the same unknown boldness that took me up the driveway, I pushed it open. I cringed as the hinges creaked – a sound which seemed to be less of a creak and more of a roar. I hid the light of my phone and held my breath, waiting for any reaction. But there was nothing.

I entered the room, praying it was V's so I didn't have to muster up the courage to head upstairs. A guilt ridden glee filled me as I found a messy bed, an unorganized computer desk, and a wall filled with posters of his favourite bands. After clearing the room, I closed the door silently by twisting the knob and guiding the door back into its frame with care. I slowly untwisted the knob, then flicked on the light. It stunned my eyes, but I couldn't let them adjust – I had to be quick.

I fired up his computer and sifted through a few drawers. The light in his bedroom seemed like a huge imposition on the rest of the house. Unlike outside, my nerves rattled and I felt wrong – like a criminal. But my body still moved, checking usual hiding places and looking everywhere for anything that could help me.

The computer finished starting up, but to my disappointment, it stopped at a login screen requesting information. Information I didn't have. I stared at it in silence.

"Routing."

My heart screamed in terror. I spun around, falling into the computer chair. It hit the desk and toppled a stack of CD cases, sending the crash of my presence through the sleeping house. I put my heart back in place, left the desk, and swiftly moved toward the sound. It had come from the bed, beneath a pile of twirled up blankets. I lifted one and there it was: the GPS system, lit up with a route mapped. It laid out directions leading north of town. To 66 OakTree Dr. I picked the device up.

"You are on the fastest route," the female voice blared. "You should reach your destination by 3:33 a.m."

My nerves trembled. Logic told me that it simply turned on and mapped it's last request. But why now?

Before I could do anything, a door slammed from upstairs. A creak followed it, then rapid footsteps. They thundered across the house toward the same stairs I had crept down moments ago. With the GPS still in hand, I got onto my stomach and rolled under the bed. The door swung open at the same time my body disappeared.

"V?" a woman asked. It was a painful question – one of senseless hope and despair. My heart sunk. It was V's mother. She hadn't seen me.

She took a few more steps in. I imagined her face – her poor distraught face – as she looked at the computer screen and open drawers. Her steps were followed by a quiet cry. She murmured through sobs her love for her son and her yearn for his return. The bed sunk as she sat down on it.

I fought off tears. Not only did her pain break my heart, but I felt like an asshole. He had told me about the door. He had asked me to join him. I could have stopped it. I could have helped him or faltered him. But I did nothing. I wanted to crawl out from underneath the bed, hug her, and tell her what I knew. But not only would that be suicide, it could potentially stop me from my investigation.

So – I thought as I looked at the GPS in my hand – I'd just have to go get him.

PART SIX

It was the third day since that night in V's basement. I went to school both days and worked the second night, though I felt like I was elsewhere the entire time. I didn't want to talk to anyone. Especially Allyster or Melissa. Or anyone else who brought up the door. They were reminders of my recklessness. But I remained content with my newfound decision to take this on by myself. Now I just needed everyone else to forget about it.

The sobs of V's mother continuously swirled through my head. It was a sound of true pain. And for two days, I did nothing about it. Perhaps it was because I feared that I'd disappear, too, if I went where the GPS wanted me to.

But I couldn't take the guilt for much longer.

It was a Wednesday night at 1 a.m. So, really, Thursday morning. I sat at my desk, the bedside lamp the only light on in my room. Outside my window – on the other side of the glass – a stillness echoed through the neighbourhood.

I needed to figure out how to get to the door.

I knew how to drive, but legally, I couldn't alone. In Ontario there are three stages to obtaining your driver's licence. The first stage is a written exam. Passing this gives you your G1. With your G1, you can operate a vehicle if a fully licensed driver of four years accompanies you. After a year of this you can take your G2 test. This is a driven test. Upon passing this you can drive alone with a few minor restrictions. After another year, you take your G test, and then you're a fully licensed driver in Ontario.

But I only had my G1 and wouldn't be getting my G2 until the summer. Despite this, I had experience behind the wheel. If I were to leave in the middle of the night, follow the rules of the road, I'd be safe. Once north of town, the chances of running into a cop were non-existent. Though, the toughest part about this plan was finding a car. I couldn't risk one of my parents waking up to the sound of their car starting, only to look out the window and see me driving away. I'd be as good as dead.

I had to be patient. My aunt and uncle lived across town. In a week they would go on their annual vacation to escape the cold. Every year, after they got into one of their two cars and drove two hours to Pearson International Airport, they left me a set of keys. My job was to water the plants and flush the toilets a few times a week to save the pipes from freezing. A car key was always left on the key ring.

I sat at my desk, my computer on. The GPS sat in front of the monitor. I found the pinpointed spot on a map. Though I planned to take the GPS with me, I wanted to mark the best – most discreet – route from their house to the country. I still couldn't risk a curious officer pulling me over.

As I was finishing up – knowing tomorrow I would curse myself for the late night – my phone vibrated. Without touching it, the lit screen revealed that it was Melissa.

My heart stuttered. I didn't want to feel that way. I barely wanted to talk to her. But I felt the warmth within my stomach. *She's texting me.* I couldn't fool myself. I knew, secretly, I did want to talk to her.

I picked it up, wondering why she was up so late.

Melissa> *Are you awake?*

I replied quickly, before she could fall asleep and forget why she ever texted me.

Dan> *Yeah.*

Melissa> *I need someone to talk to.*

Dan> *What's wrong?*

Melissa> *I got into a fight with my parents.*

I didn't know what to say, but I felt confident that I could provide some worthwhile advice if she elaborated.

Dan> *What happened?*

Melissa> *It's too long to explain over text.*

Dan> *Call me?*

Melissa> *No. I'm crying and you don't want to hear that.*

Dan> *Please don't cry. I'll come to you.*

The idea was spontaneous, but felt right. Even though I was about to crawl into bed, the butterflies she had unearthed replaced my fatigue.

Melissa> Really? *How?*

Dan> *I'll bike.*

The last two days had warmed. And by warmed, I meant -5°C instead of -20°C. I had biked in worse. Though, not as far. Melissa lived on the north point of town, up just one country road. It would take a good twenty minutes. Fifteen, if I were fast.

I pulled my jeans back on. I doubled up on socks and snuck out of the house. I wasn't going to wait for her to respond. If she said yes, I wanted to already be on my way.

I checked my phone after pulling my bike from the shed.

Melissa> *You don't have to.*

Dan> *I will. I'm on my way.*

I took off into the cold. I tried not to think about the other night. If I took the next turn, I'd be en route to V's. Would the rock move for me a second time? After listening to his mother cry for almost an hour, I had put the key back with care and returned the rock. I tore off my hat and neck gaiter and fled into the night. I broke a serious sweat hiding under that bed.

But this night was different. I journeyed into the night for me. For Melissa. I felt bad that she had gotten into a fight with her parents, but it happens. It would blow over in no time and I would be left with some serious brownie points for making an effort to be there for her. That's some class A boyfriend material.

Take that, Allyster.

The ride dragged since I had forgotten my headphones. Despite this, I made great timing. The tips of my toes and fingers were stiff and cold, but in my mind, it was worth it. I stopped at the end of her driveway and pulled one of my gloves off with my teeth, then removed my phone from my pocket.

Dan> *I'm here.*

A moment later she emerged from the back of her quiet, dark house. She wore a pair of red Roots track pants and had her hands stuffed into the pockets of a puffy black parka. Her fur-lined hood obscured her face until I met her in the middle of the driveway.

"You didn't have to come," she said. The tone of her voice seemed to accuse me of lunacy for doing what I did. But I didn't care.

"I didn't want you to be alone and crying," I replied.

She smiled.

"What happened?" I asked.

"Here," she led me to the side of the house. "We can talk in the garage where it's not freezing."

I leaned my bike against the house and followed her through a side door. She flicked a light switch which lit the room, revealing a large garage with one half dedicated to tools, boxes, and your typical garage stuff, and the other to a couch, a TV, and some tables. She moved toward the coffee table and turned on a surface heater sitting in its center. She sat on the couch in front of it. I joined her, relieved that we didn't have to talk in the cold.

We sat in silence. But it was a perfect silence. Nothing felt awkward about it. We both enjoyed the heat which met our bodies. It was a good excuse to sit nice and close to her, for the fan only heated a small area. A soft fruity smell came from her hair.

After a few moments, she fixed her posture. "My parents act like I have no say in my decisions."

"Why?"

She sighed. "My parents are great. They really are. Just sometimes, they're not," she looked at me. Right in my eyes. Even in the meek light, hers were dynamic, their colour unlike anything I'd seen before. It appeared as though a tiny green stitching held the brown of her irises together. And behind the superficial lay much more.

"What happened?" I asked, my mouth carrying out the words while my mind remained stuck in her gaze.

"I told my parents that I wanted to quit the play and they freaked."

I had forgotten about the play. The Christmas holidays extracted it from my mind and we'd only had two rehearsals since then. The teacher running it, Mrs. Dixie, had gone on vacation, so rehearsals weren't set to resume until next week. In that moment, I wanted to quit the play, too. I hardly wanted to go to school anymore and the thought of performing in front of people felt daunting now.

"Why do you want to quit?" I asked.

She shrugged, looking at the ground. "I'm not good enough."

"That's no reason to quit something," the words shot out of me. "I mean, if everyone who ever felt that they were no good simply quit, great achievers wouldn't exist."

She stared at me. I wasn't sure if my instant rejection of her statement offended her or moved her. Either way, I couldn't risk it being the former.

"Look," I continued. "Not only are you a great actor, but so many people in our school are excited to see you in the play."

She shook her head. "If I was that good, I would have gotten the lead role instead of Hannah."

I realized that since Hannah had the lead female role, and I had the lead male role, we would have to share a convincing fake kiss. How great would it have been if Melissa *did* get the lead female role?

I didn't tell her why I shared in her disappointment, but a part of me now did. I had been far too thrilled when Mrs. Dixie cast me as lead, and since I'd anticipated getting the role, I didn't consider how it'd feel to not get it. The class had sat around in a circle in the drama room waiting to hear the cast list. After a week of auditions, we would finally know. We chatted nervously, yet optimistically about which role we would get. When the teacher finally walked in, it switched to the silence of a chapel holding a funeral. Mrs. Dixie cleared her throat and went down the list. People jumped up, rocking a fist upon hearing their role, while others tried to hold it together before leaving in tears. I was among the former. I never thought about how it would have felt to be the latter.

"That is a bummer," I paused. "But Mrs. Dixie does the play every year and she's good when it comes to casting. I know she didn't decide to not give you lead because of what you lacked, but because of what you could bring to the table for the character you *were* cast for. Which, in itself, is a pretty big role."

"I know, you're right. And I'd otherwise be happy, but..." her eyes looked around the room while she searched for words. "Wherever we go, everyone fascinates about how Hannah is the lead and how amazing that is. I feel so left out. I know it's stupid..."

Before I could reply, she digressed.

"And so my parents freaked on me. They went on yelling at me that I'm a quitter, how I'll just go on to quit everything, and how nobody loves a quitter. Like, who says that? Who implies that they don't love their own daughter?"

She had me there. "Maybe they were having a bad day?"

"I don't know," she sighed. "Whatever, I just can't wait until I can go off to school next year."

She leaned into me and hugged me. "You're so great for coming all this way to see me."

I hugged her back. Maybe it was a superfluous act just to soothe the frustration of an argument, but biking to her felt right. And hugging her felt even more right. I held onto her, trying to grasp the moment so I'd be able to capture it later with ease. But by doing so, I let the hug pass sans satisfaction.

She pulled away. "Remember in Tim Horton's when you told me you liked me?"

I nodded.

"It's not that I don't like you back," she said. "I just... can't."

"Why not?"

"It wouldn't be fair to Allyster," she paused. "He likes me too."

"Do you like him?"

A long pause. "No."

I didn't want to ask if she liked me. I'd much rather pretend she did than ask and find out for sure. Making her decide so soon could seal a deal that didn't have to be finalized yet.

It all ended abruptly when she told me that she needed to go back inside. I hugged her goodbye and the next thing I knew I was back out in the cold astride on my bike.

I watched the garage light flick off. A brisk, weighty wind messed my hair. I coasted down her driveway, fully intending on heading south, back into town.

But then it occurred to me. I was already north of town. Getting so close to Melissa had woken me up, and I didn't want to go back home to bed. I didn't have the GPS, but something told me I was close and could find the door on my own. So, instead, I went north. I left the row of houses which made up Melissa's street and started down a random country road.

That bike ride was unlike anything I had ever experienced. Something filled me. It felt like that warm fuzzy feeling alcohol provides. But just that small tinge and nothing else. There was no dizziness. No poor logic. Though, I did seem far too poised with my journey. My mindset had instinctively transitioned to one of confidence, my body taking turns and going down roads as though I were headed somewhere I'd been a hundred times.

The sureness and comfort stopped faster than I could hit the brakes and halt my bike. Suddenly, pain from the cold struck my hands and feet. I was out in the woods all alone, stopped in the middle of an old road. The darkness surrounded me and the silence was nauseating. I shivered and pulled out my phone. It was dead.

How long had I been biking for? My cell had been plugged in at my house and it had a near full charge when I'd left for Melissa's. Suddenly, I realized I could hardly remember much after I had turned off of Melissa's road. Hardly anything except for the blur of trees and that euphoric feeling.

I took a look around. My eyes were well adjusted to the moonlight. To my right, an ATV path stemmed off of the road. The adjoining path was small and dense. *Like a tunnel into the thickets.* Two looming oak trees guarded each side of the entrance. Somehow, I knew what waited down there. And I knew I had to go in. I wouldn't be able to live with myself if I turned around and... tried to go home.

The cries of V's mother fell from the trees – a subtle reverberation coming from above, just like the other night. I remained on the road for a moment, blocking it out. I didn't require a recap. The guilt already lived in my mind. But I did need some mental preparation before heading down that path. If my heart pumped any faster, it was sure to explode. Though, its power was the only thing warming me against the baleful cold. It did not feel like a mere -5°C anymore.

I finally told myself that I couldn't wait any longer. I kicked off and coasted down the unknown road. Thoughts filled my head as I biked upon the icy gravel. I worried that it wouldn't even be the right road. Maybe it was just a farmer's driveway. Or maybe the door truly did wait at the end. And I would wind up like V. Gone without a trace, my bike in the No Frills' parking lot.

The path was icy and bumpy – a difficult terrain for bicycle tires – but the journey ended quickly. I stopped at the sight of it. The moon came through the trees, lighting the door with purpose. Even with my distance, the details were clear. Dark weathered wood, constructed by vertical two-by-sixes, were cut at the top to fit an arched frame. The knob was like a large brown mushroom growing out of the right side. And the hinges grabbed onto the first two-by-six on the left, looking like sideways pitch forks.

I stared in disbelief. V had been here. It could even be the last place he had seen before he...

The chilling thought snapped me back into reality – the reality of my solitude in the winter woods. The silence haunted me. My breath – bringing a brief mist before me – seemed a bother to the still and silent scene. Perhaps I, too, came off as a bother to it all.

I dropped my bike and approached it. I moved off of the road and took a few steps into the forest before I stood in front of the door. The oak tree V had mentioned shot out of the top and towered above the other trees. The earth around the door's rocky border seemed fresh – clean of snow and unfrozen. And the air before it felt warm. Too warm for a January night. Its relief drew me in like a passerby seeking refuge from a storm.

I saw the key hole beneath the handle and hoped V had left it unlocked. The fingers beneath my gloves were numb and pained, the vessels within them constricted. Still, I used whatever strength remained in them to grip the knob. It turned fully. There came a click. Then the hinges creaked as I pushed open the door.

When my foot moved through the threshold of the door, the entire atmosphere changed. The air turned warm and dry. Soft heat breezed from the darkness before me. Nearly frozen to death, it drew me in.

Once fully inside, the door slammed shut, leaving me in darkness. The obscurity comforted me, seemingly trying to ease me into a sleep or trance. It was like my nighttime bedroom back in the days before fear haunted it. But I couldn't shut down. I couldn't sleep. I would be left vulnerable to whatever loitered in the blackness. So, instead, I stood for a moment. Many moments. Ones in which all I could do was ponder in the darkness. Time vanished – no longer a factor. I could have stood there for five seconds or a thousand years. I still don't know. For it didn't matter. Behind the door, they were both the same.

I blinked, suddenly a bit more lucid. The air had turned still, yet remained warm. It was cozy, like Allyster's apartment.

A panic began as soon as that thought ended. The calmness departed. Reality snapped fully back into place. It occurred to me that I may never again set foot in Allyster's apartment if I stayed where I was. Clearly V had nothing to do with this. He came, found an empty dark room, and left.

My arm reached back for the knob, but it hit dirt. I swung around and pressed both hands into the earth. It felt warm, like a brownie-filled pan fresh from the oven. And that's all I found. I felt across the wall – left a few steps, then right – but the door had vanished.

"No," I breathed.

My dirt covered hands trembled. My heart fought to escape my chest just as I did with the room. But we were both stuck.

I turned back toward the darkness. There had to be another way out. I had to escape. But before I could take a single step and begin my journey, an illumination shook upon the walls. The flicker of a light – so dull it could have been mistaken as trickery of the eye – ambled within the blackness. It was a dot floating a couple of car lengths away.

When I had first entered high school, I found myself the victim of sleep paralysis on numerous occasions. This is a phenomenon in which one awakens with the inability to move. This includes speaking – and for grade nine me –

screaming. Often, during these bouts, people see *things*. For me, it was a dark mist. I would lay there with no choice but to stare at whatever this horrid mist might have been. As I read up on it, I found that some believe sleep paralysis to be a demonic visitation. This is my experience with it. Because it wasn't just about what I saw, but what I felt. Something foul lingered in my bedroom and with it came an intense fear. One so terrifying that, if I'd had my body at my command, I would have sent it running through the nearest door.

That's what accompanied this light. The epitome of evil living through a tiny glow. As it approached, the miasmal essence intensified, dripping from the glow and into the air. I cowered against the dirt, hardly noticing its approach. But its light eventually illuminated my trembling body. I looked to see that what was once a pin prick in the darkness was now a flame sitting atop a candle stick. A candle clasped by two hands. V's hands.

"V?" I shuddered. "Why? Why are you still here? You need to come home."

I looked into his eyes. They looked at me as though to seek a reaction. The sinister feeling faded, but with it, something remained. Something, too, that adored evil.

"Dan, you came," he said with a smile.

"How have you been living here?" I tried to look past him. But all was black minus a sudden wall to the right of us – one I swore popped into existence right at that moment. On it, a sort of clay was pressed into the dirt. Dozens of red names filled its surface. Each one had an arrow swooping down to the next. When the names met the floor, an arrow stretched from the bottom to the top, connecting the names. The last two signatures were *Kate* followed by *Mike*.

"You received my messages," he replied.

I didn't know what to say to him. My mind struck back to his mother crying. He was missing voluntarily, causing pain to his friends and family without a care. And for some reason, my mouth only sent him one question.

"Why is your car still at the store?"

He barely reacted. "It happens differently for everyone."

I stared at him. He wasn't who he was before. He might have been in there, but he was different.

"What do you mean?"

"When you go looking for the door," he nearly cut me off. "You find it. You may be sitting in your car in a parking lot, planning to map out your way," he looked up into the blackness. "You're all alone. There's no one around. Next thing you know, you look up from your phone, and there it is."

"The door?"

He nodded and looked at the wall of names. "And now that you're here, it's time for you to make a wish."

"A wish?" I stared at him, dumbfounded. "For what?"

"Anything you want," he said. "See, I made a mistake. I wished for invisibility. Problem is, I can't control it. It's not like the Ring of Gyges. I'm *always* invisible. Outside of the door, I can hardly touch or hold anything. No one can see *nor* hear me. Truly, I am invisible. But only one person can carry a wish at a time. So, once you wish, mine will be lifted. I will be able to return to my family again."

"And what about me?" I asked.

He seemed eager. In a way, I didn't blame him. But his tone was pushy. And still, something foreboding loomed.

"You, well," he laughed quickly. "You get to go home too. With your wish. Just word it better than I did."

"Who?" I stammered. "Who grants these?"

His face went deadpan. "Worry not who grants this."

I retracted, pressing myself against where I wished the door was. Like a breeze, the evil aura returned with tenfold the force of what it is was before. V changed, grunting and baring his teeth. His face twitched and he roared like a beast in agony.

"Make a wish," a demonic voice pierced the cries.

"No," I sunk lower with nowhere to run. The petit light flickered uncontrollably in his hands.

"Dan!" a voice pleaded.

It was V's voice. The one that would crack jokes with me at work in the back room when we should have been working. But his face looked demented and wicked. I pushed back farther against the wall, fear eating away at me. And the wall gave. With a long creak, I fell backward into the snow. But – even with the dead, winter forest around me – the snow was warm like the wall, the air like a summer night.

The open door stood before me, the oak tree towering over it. I pushed my-self back, that light shimmering in the doorway's center. The howls of V escaped into the woods. But still, the guy I knew cried:

"Help me."

I watched him step out of the door. Despite his cry, he ignored me. A fight was happening. Different roars and screams left the same man. But they faded as another noise overtook them.

My ringtone.

Somehow, my dead phone rang. I reached for it, prompting V's body to come at me in long strides.

"No," it yelled.

On the ground, I pulled out my phone and looked at it. My heart sank. It was still dead. But the ringing continued. It drowned out everything.

"Back inside we go," he yelled.

V grabbed the wrist which held the phone, pulling me up. His grip burned, cauterizing my skin, sizzling even through the phone's ring. I dropped my cell, face to face with the estranged V.

But a quick shift came upon the man's face.

"Run," V whimpered.

Then everything faded. I felt nothing, saw nothing. Only the sound of my phone remained. The terrible presence faded. My head hurt. I lifted my neck to look at my phone screen. It lay beside me in the snow, still ringing. It was my mom. The screen brought a light which – to my fragile eyes – equated to the beam of an Acura's brights. The parts of my body that I could feel were stiff. The others were numb from the cold. I tried to grab my phone, but could bare-ly control my arms and hands. I struggled to get up, pushing the bike I hadn't realized was on top of me to the side.

My phone stopped ringing. I had twenty-six missed calls and forty-seven texts. I looked around for the door, but it was nowhere. I was in a ditch. The cold was eating at my body. I shook my limbs as the rate of my heart picked up, placing an even larger strain on it. I crawled out of the snow-filled ditch and as close to the road as I could. Headlights emerged from the distance. The last thing I remembered was waiting for the beacon of light to save me before I lost consciousness.

• • • •

I SUFFERED HYPOTHERMIA and frostbite that night. Though this is a terrible pair, they were both mild cases. The doctors assured me that I was extremely fortunate to have such a circumstance. The couple that picked me up, by luck, recognized my symptoms and carefully loaded me into their vehicle. My mom happened to call again once they did. She was finally met with a response when the woman picked up and told her the situation and that they were headed for the hospital.

I stayed there for a few days before heading home.

• • • •

DESPITE THE HAUNTING memory of that night, things seemed to be going well. I had the week off of school and didn't mind doing my homework via e-mails in between Warcraft time. The frostbite I acquired from falling unconscious in the ditch was healing nicely, though the doctor warned me quite extensively that the tissue had undergone damage which could become permanent if it saw the cold again for a prolonged period of time.

Melissa and I were in constant text mode. We would text until we fell asleep, carrying on the conversation the next morning. It became such a norm to my day that I felt its absence when she was unable to use her phone when she went to work. And this communication brought us closer. If it weren't for the Allyster thing she had told me the night of the incident, I'm certain we'd be dating. That's how it felt to me, anyway. We'd send hearts, say goodnight, and we were there for each other. Looking back, it sounds juvenile, but to 2010 me, it meant a lot.

Though, things weren't all chocolate and rainbows. For one, there were the dreams. Or, night terrors, rather. V was there. The voice was there. It was always them, the candle, the list, and the darkness. I couldn't escape it. The dream would never end early. I was destined to carry out whatever my conscious streamed to me. But I never felt alone. I always sensed someone's presence when I woke. And then I'd lay there, looking upon my empty room, eerily wondering if V had come to visit me.

The dreams were awful, but they seemed a distant problem come daytime. Even with the constant reminder of the burn on my wrist. My excuse was that I didn't know how it got there. The doctor explained it away as an ice burn, isolated for one reason or another. And I could almost buy that one if it weren't for the dreams and the feeling of a presence.

Every morning, I would go downstairs and sit for breakfast with my family. And that was the second shadow cast over the chocolate rainbow. My family had been overly nice to me. Even my sister, who I had never really built a solid relationship with, sent me bundles of kindness. And as great as this was, we never talked about *the incident.* That elephant floated around the room, occasionally tapping into us and sticking to our hair like a balloon. But we'd push it away. Every time. I had no grand excuse for what I had been doing out on my bike that night and I had the full intention of telling the truth – minus the door of course – were they to ask. But no one ever asked. And I didn't want to be the one to bring it up. Maybe they had the same rationale, but wouldn't they want to know? Why didn't they just ask?

Well, finally, my mom called me downstairs two nights before I was due back at school. I made my way down the stairs, my foot finally healed, save for a scar. I turned the corner into the living room and there they were: Mom and Dad on the couch, ready for a serious talk. I sat down on the chair across from them. If I played victim and kept my role as the good Samaritan being there for a girl he liked, I'd have the sympathy to escape this with not even a slap on the wrist. All I had to do was tell the truth – or half of it.

But they didn't ask where I had gone that night. What they asked was much worse.

"Dan," my mother stared into my eyes. "Why did you sneak into Mike Veller's house last week?"

PART EIGHT

It only took once to burn my dad. First impressions stuck to him. If you had B.O. the first time you met my dad, you can bet your last rock that he would forever think of you as the stinky one. Even if you stunk on the third time meeting him, he might just brand you and leave it at that. It was his way. If he had a Buick and it broke down, then that was that. Buicks sucked forever, all around. It was a fallacy, I know, but perhaps he found it easier to assess things once and be done with it.

I had previously been classified as his run-of-the-mill son – nothing too special about that kid, but also nothing all that wrong. I was sure of this evaluation. But sitting in the living room that day, I got re-evaluated. Branded once again. Because if you did something which shook my dad's assessment hard enough, he'd – without much thought – just slide you into a different drawer. And my new drawer had the words *bad teenager* written upon it.

My mom ran her fingernail along the stitching of the couch while she tried hard to keep eye contact with me. She was nervous. As was I. My dad sat beside her on the loveseat like he was listening to a preacher at church. Slouched, he had his arms crossed, his eyes fiercely trying to burn holes into the carpet. I hoped he thought that I had a more prosaic reason for what I did and that – after hearing my excuse – he would know I wasn't some sort of criminal.

But *Coming Up With Excuses Under Pressure* wasn't a card I was dealt or one I had ever picked up from the deck. As it turned out, a criminal was exactly how they both viewed me. And I don't blame the one who brought this to their attention. I ran out of V's house that night like it had gone ablaze, ripping off my hat and neck gaiter in a panic. Now that I think about it, it was as stupid a move as leaving my wallet behind. Because the people who lived across the street from V and his family just so happened to know my parents. And when one of them saw me from out their front window – awake for God knows what reason – they knew it was me. They held their tongue for a painful amount of time, and then told my parents instead of V's so as to save the Veller's the extra burden.

Now the problem lay in my parent's hands and I had absolutely no idea what to say.

"Um, I..." stupidly spilled out of my mouth, even though I knew my repute was contingent on this excuse. "He borrowed something of mine and I wanted it back."

I'm stupid. I know. I was hoping we could just leave it at that – it really did seem ingenious at the time – but...

"And what might this something be?"

"A GPS," I answered truthfully – half truthfully. It may not have been the brightest answer, but I did indeed bring one out of his house. It was the only bit of legitimacy I had to the story.

"Why do you have or even need a GPS?" she fired back.

My dad remained in his position, his head nodding slightly. I think that's when my heart sunk the most. I realized that my dad indeed thought of me as a thief. One trying to take advantage of someone who had gone missing. But I couldn't respond. I didn't know how. I was caught and there was no way I could explain the door to them.

"Well," my mom stood up. "You're grounded until you tell us the truth."

She walked out of the room. My dad glanced up at me right after she left. He didn't need to hold his look for long. I could tell it was one of pure disappointment. One of a successful re-examination of his son.

The kid? Nothing good. He's all bad.

It wrung my heart of blood and filled it back up with a mixture of sorrow, embarrassment, and regret. Then he left.

• • • •

THE SCAR ON MY ARM had been healing quickly, and once it was no more than a flush blemish, I began to doubt the reality of my experience behind the apparent door.

But then night came and with them the dreams...

During the daytime, however, it was all a faraway concept, like wars in countries overseas that can be turned off with the click of a TV remote.

The first time I was somewhat confronted with it during the day was on my first morning back at school. It was only a Friday, so as to ween me back into being mobile again. I was excited to get back to see everyone – especially Melissa. She hadn't texted me back since that night my parents grounded me, and I needed to know why. I had told her I had gotten into a fight with *my* parents, and that was the end of it.

But she wasn't who I saw first. Allyster came through the collection of morning students and right up to me the moment I entered the school.

"What were you doing out in those woods north of town, man?" he asked. His eyes seemed to have little invisible arms that grabbed me and slammed me against a locker. I chuckled, but his concerned face stuck, like from a photograph, and I wondered if he knew the truth – if Melissa had told him.

I also thought of where lies and half-truths had gotten me.

"I was biking back from Melissa's," I told him. "I tried to take a quicker route home, but got lost."

It was a half-truth before I even knew it. He frowned and flicked his head in question. "What were you doing out there so late on a Wednesday?"

"She got into a fight with her parents. She was upset, so I went to talk it out with her."

"Gotcha," he said, his eyes round and brows raised. "I gotta get to class, dude. I'll catch you later."

Before I could reply, he walked off, shoulders hunched.

Allyster was the only one to ask questions. Everyone else simply told me that they were glad to have me back. The consensus was that I'd been biking, came upon some ice, fell into the ditch, and hit my head on the way down. And as the story went, I *was* biking home from Melissa's. Allyster knew the truth, but he wanted to hear it straight from the horse's mouth. Gratefully, I had told him.

Or, mostly.

I spent the majority of my time outside of class looking for Melissa. I had seen her once, far up the hallway, but couldn't catch up to her in the crowd. She was around, just not responding to my texts. But she couldn't ignore me the entire day. Play rehearsal was that evening.

· · · ·

I DON'T WANT TO NAME the play for which we were rehearsing, because I don't want to draw attention to the school or the town which endured the horrendous series of events I had caused them. I have done enough to disrupt the lives of the underserving people who were not involved, yet affected. All I'll say is that it was a whodunit.

By the time practice neared, I felt too anxious to worry about the dress rehearsal of the first two acts. Even though it was a hefty question of whether or not my foot could handle the strain it would take to run all those scenes, I couldn't get my mind off of Melissa's virtual silence.

Either way, when I entered backstage, I was glad to see excited faces greeting me.

"You can do it, Dan," a girl said and patted my foot with a chuckle.

"We can switch if you want," a guy who had the part of a one-minute walk-on joked.

Others waved and gave thumbs up. It relieved my anxiety nicely.

"Hey," Eric came up to me as my eyes floated around the room of people getting in costume, putting on make-up, setting up props. "How's the foot? Still good to go?"

"Yeah, I can do it," I said. "Is everyone here for the dress rehearsal?"

Eric nodded. "Yeah. Your new girlfriend is out at a table talking to Allyster."

"She's not my girlfriend," I said, wishing I didn't have to, hoping that the opposite could be true. "I'll be back in a sec to get ready."

I left Eric and went around the set, onto the stage. Hannah was hanging a poster – a prop – onto a post. She glanced over at me as I came onto the set. Without a word, she went back to her task.

Melissa and Allyster sat at a table – one of the ones that could and would be converted into a bench for the show. Allyster noticed me first, looking quickly away and blatantly telling Melissa that I had seen them. She, too, glanced up.

I hate confrontation, but I had to act for nearly two hours starting in five minutes and I knew I couldn't do that without some sort of answer. I went down the stairs and into the audience toward them. Melissa whispered a few things to Allyster, got up, and started toward me.

"Hey," I said once she was close enough.

Before I could ask her why I hadn't heard from her in days – after nearly two weeks of non-stop text conversation – she asked me something which generally meant bad news in these scenarios.

"Can we talk about something?"

"Sure," I said, my anxiety back in action.

We walked into the corner of the venue, beside the emergency exit.

"What is it?" I asked.

"I just don't think that we should mislead people," she paused as I stared with inquisitive eyes. "People are saying all sorts of things as to why you were at my house that night. People think we had sex. They think we're dating."

"Who cares what they think?" I said. "And besides, is that so bad? I thought you said you liked me?"

"It was late, I..." she paused again. "I don't know how I feel."

She glanced behind my shoulder to where I knew Allyster was sitting.

"I didn't tell people those things," I said. "I haven't told anyone anything. I only told Allyster that I was coming back from your house because he asked. All I told him was the truth."

Her eyes became a little more forgiving. "You didn't text me about you and your parents fighting to get me to come to your house?"

"What? No," I shook my head. "My parents and I *are* fighting. I'm grounded. They hate me right now. Especially my dad..."

"I'm sorry," she said.

"I promise I'm not spreading stuff or trying to pull a fast one, okay?" I said, knowing I might still be able to get back into her good books. Her *I might like you* books.

"Dan," she said. "You were found farther north than my house. And from what I've heard, much later than the time you left my house. Where were you biking to, really?"

I wanted to spill it all right there. To tell her everything and get her on my side – to help against my parents who thought of me as a delinquent, to help me find V, to help clear away all of the confusion. I knew I needed help, but...

"Everyone ready in two minutes," Mrs. Dixie called.

I looked to the stage, then back at Melissa.

"Look," I said. "I really need to talk to you about something serious."

She nodded, her face stern.

"I'm grounded probably for the rest of my life, but tomorrow my parents are going out of town – something for my mom's work. Could we possibly meet somewhere during the day? When there's more time?"

"Okay," she agreed, her eyes worried.

• • • •

THE DRESS REHEARSAL went well – likely due to the fact that some life had been brought back into me after having talked to Melissa – and my foot put on the performance of its life. The rest of the evening at home was less pleasant. My parents still wanted the truth, but the truth was substantially more preposterous than the half-truth I had given them. If I went the extra length and told them that the ghost of V, or invisible V, or what-have-you V was communicating with me from beyond a ghoulish door, I would probably be spending my summer vacation around a bunch of psychiatrists.

Either way, it was Friday night and I was home. The nightmares had become about every other night. I even went through a three-night period where I didn't have a nightmare at all. But something about that Friday night felt foreboding, like dark clouds making their way across an ocean toward shore.

I did what I had done each night that week and settled into bed especially early. It was best to get to sleep while the rest of the house kept awake with its usual noises; the TV mumbling the news, the kitchen tap coming on, a door closing. That way the fear couldn't bite me. They always warned of bedbugs at bedtime, but never of the fear. Fear was the real culprit – *it* was the real thing that would infest you as you and all else slept.

So, I had to beat that era of the night with the life and the light from the rest of the house. Though, while my mind played the script of what I planned to say to Melissa, I worried it'd be many hours before I found sleep.

The note.

Then the message on the wall.

The GPS.

The door.

Over and over in my head. But within it, time leapt. The hallway light was on – a slice of radiance between my bed and the window – the TV acted out some scene with muffled voices, my dad coughed, the microwave beeped. Then all in a motion I couldn't comprehend – within a subtle stir – all fell dark and silent. January wind brushed up against my window with a hollow whistle.

I blinked and looked around my dark room, a colder and stranger place than a mere moment ago. It lay dead quiet, made up of shadows and shapes and *anything your mind wanted them to be, really.*

Bzzt Bzzt.

Light cast upon the ceiling. It was the candle. V's candle. Except it wasn't V. Something had taken him over. And now it stood in my room, here to finish the deed.

Make a wish, it said.

I sat up. Emptiness. Silence. No one had said anything. A gust of wind hit my window, gently rattling the glass as if to laugh. But that was all.

My cell phone had gone off. It occurred to me that that was likely what had woken me up. I reached for it. The time was 1:22 a.m. Melissa had texted me.

Melissa> *Look what we found!*

Below this was a file name with the option to download it.

Melissa> *Picture/Video File. <Download>*

I hit the button with no hesitation. My hands began to tremble. My heart – gently beating as I slept moments ago – now fired in my chest. I sat up fully as I watched the image download. I already knew what it was going to show me. I prayed furiously in that moment that it would be anything else. But, finally, a picture of Allyster beside the door – the one I had witnessed myself – popped up on my screen. He stood proudly beside it, a goofy smile on his face, both of his thumbs up.

I shot out of bed, my body shaking. They didn't understand what they had just found. I had let it all get too out of hand. I grabbed the GPS from my desk drawer. I fled down the stairs like a ghost, grabbed the keys to my aunt and uncle's car, then left the house. Underdressed for the winter night, I burst down the icy driveway on my bike.

PART NINE

My aunt had a white 2009 GMC Acadia. That was the car that waited for me. It had navigation, leather seats, a sunroof, all that fun stuff. Gratefully, it also had heat, for my foot – along with every exposed part of my body – was beginning to ache from the deadly wind.

I neared their house and started to coast, my bike's derailleur clacking. Dread filled me as I stared at their approaching home. They never left. The whole thing was foiled. I had to either give up and go home – retire from the nonsense with the door and the damage I had done – or bike to the location with the GPS as my guide, the risk of losing my foot great.

I stopped the bike with a small squeal of the brakes, a sound quickly carried away by the wind. The living room light illuminated the blue curtains which hung before the window. The small square window a few feet above the front door was also lit up. It was their upstairs bathroom.

They were home.

And also up late.

I sat there for any other nocturnal neighbours to see and eventually expose me to my parents. I watched, wondering how I had made such a mistake – wondering what, if anything, I could do. The bathroom light went off. Cold wind blew at me, burrowing into my numb ears. I covered them with my hands, trying to figure out how I didn't know that they had stayed.

A light on the side of the house came on, illuminating the bushes which ran along their property. And with that lightbulb, one came on in my head. I knew what was going on. We wouldn't have their keys had they stayed.

Someone had broken into their house. Not that night, but years ago, while they were on their trip – I believe that year it was Mexico. Two men had broken into their dark and obviously empty house. Since then, they had installed automatic lights. Throughout the night, these lights turned themselves on and off, usually changing once every few hours so as to make it look like someone was home – and up all night, I suppose. That tactic, along with their neighbour's watchful eyes and collection of their mail, had kept their home safe from thieves.

Until now.

I shook my head, pushing that last thought away. I wasn't a thief. I was family, simply borrowing something for an hour or so.

"Nothing wrong with it," I said to the wind, then headed up the driveway. I sat astride on my bike as I entered their garage code. It opened with silence. I leaned my bike up against the wall inside, unlocked the SUV, and hopped inside. The seat was cold and stiff. I started it and the car fired up like the engine was already warm.

Rod Stewart's "You Wear It Well" played on the radio, which was tuned into the local rock station. I turned it off. I needed to concentrate. I grabbed the wheel and looked forward, noticing that the headlights were fixed on the front window of a house across the street, the Acadia having been backed in. I couldn't let that happen for too long. I pressed the brake, shifted the car into drive, and let it roll down the driveway. I pressed one of the buttons on the remote attached to the sun visor and happily watched the garage door roll close in the rear-view mirror.

"You are on the fastest route. You should reach your destination by 1:57 a.m."

The sound blared from my pocket – the speaker on it causing a small vibration against my leg. I removed the GPS, momentarily perplexed by how it knew I was ready to go. But high strangeness was becoming a norm around here.

I placed the device in the cup holder so that it faced me, turned up the heat, and pulled out of the driveway.

• • • •

I HAD NEVER TEXTED Melissa back, though it probably would have been the best move to text or call and warn them about the door. But when this realization hit, it was already too late.

Heat now filled the car as I headed down a country road, one that turned off of the main stretch which ran through the northern part of town. All of the roads were clean and clear, but it appeared that – were I to encounter the road again – it might be tough to enter it given the surrounding snowbanks.

"In 300 metres, turn right," the GPS said.

My heart accelerated. I slowed down, keeping an eye out for Melissa's Volvo. Again, I felt shaky and...

My eyes shot to the rear-view mirror.

There's someone in here, I thought, looking at the rear seat headrests.

"Re-routing," the GPS announced.

I jumped. Sweat ran from my hairline. I turned down the heat that I had wished for so greatly on my bike ride and looked down at the GPS.

"In 500 metres, make a U-turn," it said.

The little arrow which represented me in my aunt's car spun to the left, then to the right.

"Re-routing," it repeated.

I stopped the car, put it in park, and grabbed the GPS.

"Stay on Ontario Highway 401 west for 828 kilometers."

"What the...?" I mumbled.

I tried moving it around in an eight to try and help it find its location. But the thing was broken, lost itself. I looked down at it, anger swelling inside of me, and I thought briefly of calling Melissa. If I were close, maybe she could help me get to them.

"Your destination is on the right," the GPS sounded. The arrow now sat in the middle of a white blank screen, save for the words *66 OakTree Dr.* in the top left corner.

I looked up. It was true. No longer did I sit on the road, but a snowy trail – one so deep, I worried that the Acadia wouldn't be able to get back out. To the right, off into the woods a bit, the door and its surrounding dirt stuck out against the snow.

My eyes scanned the area for Melissa or Allyster. Or even their footprints. But there seemed to be no indication that they had actually been there. I pulled out my phone and texted her like I originally should have.

Dan> *Where are you?*

I sat with my phone in my hand, my heart hammering in my chest, waiting for something to jump up by my window. But the scene outside seemed to not be a scene at all, just a picture – a moment frozen in time. I pressed the brake pedal to try and find some shapes in the darkness that the mirrors showed me. Red glowing trees surrounded the back of the vehicle, save for the skinny snow-covered path I was apparently supposed to reverse out of.

I contemplated trying to leave. To leave and never come to the door again. For the door seemed enticing throughout the day. Even sometimes at night. Like a pending adventure. Something drew you toward it. Not so much in the way of a possession, but more like the way pilgrims venture to holy sites. Coming to the door felt obligatory, as though life's secrets hid behind its wooden boards.

But I knew what was in there.

Darkness.

A wall of names.

A possessed V.

Then dread, fear, and regret filled you upon finding the door. Your innate instincts instructed you to flee. But, you didn't. Curiosity overrode common sense. Like I did in that moment, sitting in my aunt's SUV, I felt like I owed it to myself to do what I came to do – whatever that might have been.

I killed the engine and got out of the car, sinking into a foot of snow. I had forgotten how cold it was outside. But the coldness here felt different. The frigid air stood still. And it wasn't the trees sheltering me from the wind. The air, though terribly cold, did not waver. My breath moved into it, then fell still itself.

I walked around the vehicle, my footsteps loud in the silence. The car's engine quietly clicked and clacked behind me.

Bzzt.

Melissa> *We're at Allyster's. That place was too creepy.*

I stared at my screen. I had come for nothing. My talk with her tomorrow would be moot. She chose Allyster over me. Allyster chose her over me. I stared at the text, my heart feeling as though it were peeling and dropping into my stomach. Despondent and angry, I planned to run through the door and tell whatever lived there to give me its best.

"Dan?"

I looked up, my eyes shooting from the brightness of my phone. I squinted, trying to mentally push away the green blob which blocked my sight.

"Who?" I stammered.

Footsteps approached from the direction of the door. I blinked viciously. And all at once, my vision cleared and he came into view.

"V?" I said, stepping back.

"Dan," he came closer. "I promise that it's me. It can't leave the door," he glanced back at it. "At least not physically."

"Who can't?" I asked, then quickly added. "How did you get... free?"

"A girl and a guy were here," he said. "She went inside. She made a wish and the wish freed me."

"What are you talking about?"

"A wish," he said. "It takes your soul for a wish. He leads people here, takes the form of a human – usually – then trades your soul for a wish."

Even after all I had seen and heard, I felt that V had lost it – rambling about wishes and souls.

"But he will negotiate," he continued, motioning back at the door as if he were doing a documentary special on a passed loved one and this was their grave and this was their story. "If you try and get someone else to come and make a wish, he gives you back your soul, takes back your wish, and deals with the new-comer."

"And," I mumbled, still unsure of whether or not I believed him. "Melissa?"

"Yeah, that was her name," V said. "It's in there, on the wall..."

"It has her soul?"

"Yeah. I wished for invisibility, but it went wrong. I was always invisible. I couldn't be seen, heard, or felt. I'm sorry I tried to get you to come make a wish, but I..."

I started in the snow, passing him.

"Where are you going?"

"To kill two birds with one stone," I said.

"No," he started after me, pulling on my sweater. "You can't go in there. You don't know what it is."

I shrugged him off, opened the door, and went inside.

• • • •

I HAD UNDOUBTEDLY SCREWED up many things up to this point. I had done many things I still regret. But it was in this moment – this night –

that the larger mistakes had begun. The ones which terrorized many people in my otherwise sleepy town. The ones which ruined the future for myself and many others. The ones that, once I did, there was no turning back. And please keep in mind that I was younger when this story took place. Lost in many ways, I didn't know how to guide myself or my decisions. This story has been hard to recount the way I have here. It took substantially longer to write this than it will for anyone to read it. But it must be written. Or the universe will forget. There will be no conscious memory of me, the others, or how it all happened.

On this night I triggered the sequence of horrors which followed, including my dreadful fate.

I found myself in the darkness once again. V's protests vanished when I stepped inside. The door closed behind me, sucked into the wall. A lantern sat burning on a table a few steps ahead of me. Mike ⇨ Melissa – along with all the other names – were written in red on the wall to the right of it. She had really done it.

Beside the lantern lay a red utensil.

What neither Melissa nor I knew at the time was that with the trading of your soul, there comes great consequence. The research I've done since then leaves me to believe that the reason is this: when you're a body without a soul, things seek you out. You're an empty container and entities out in the many planes – or what have you – yearn for a container to call home. So, without a soul, one is in the company of others. One is haunted.

It was the hauntings I was unknowingly trying to save Melissa from, though I ended up signing her up for something much worse.

"I'm here to make a wish," I called.

My voice rang into the darkness beyond the lantern's light, into the seemingly endless void of the room. But there came no response. No emergence of any figure – not one of Melissa, though a morbid part of me had hoped there would be – came from the black part of the...

Cave?

Tunnel?

Just a voice. But this voice didn't ring out such as mine had. It sounded in my head, much the same as a thought, but not my own. Its soothing voice, dragging softly from word to word, told me to make my wish, then mark my name.

"I wish..." I started.

I looked at all of the names and noticed that they were all unique – written by different hands. I walked up and grabbed the utensil, which was like a large pencil crayon. Beside Melissa's name an arrow I hadn't noticed before curved down to the blank area beneath her name – her name which she had written herself with the very pencil I held.

"I wish Melissa hated Allyster," I declared to the dark place, then scribbled my name.

PART TEN

What I realize now is that I had wished for negativity. What might have created a better situation was if I had wished for Melissa to love me. But I had been angry, distraught, and I had wished for something worse. Something which may not have affected me in any way, as I had no part in the actual wish itself. I was concerned with tearing others down when I should have been trying to build myself up.

But, luckily, the wish did – at first – work in my favour.

Melissa had stopped talking to Allyster. In turn, she had started talking to me. A lot. And it didn't take long once I had made the wish.

After I wrote my name down on the wall, I woke up to a humming noise. The wish had felt like a dream, however the moment in which reality slipped into the dream was unclear. I knew I had taken my aunt's car and driven out to the door. I had seen and talked to V. I had gotten upset by Melissa's text.

I had made the wish.

There was a hard bump. I realized that I was laying on a cushioned surface. I lifted my head to see a dark highway illuminated by headlights. V's head shot toward the back seat where I sat. He was driving my aunt's SUV.

"Thank God you're up," he said. "I wasn't sure what happened, I just..." he looked back out the windshield. We were driving down the main route which would take us into town.

"You came in through the door with me?"

"Dan, I'd never go back in there," he said. "I pulled your arm as you went inside and dragged you out before you could fully get in. Then you hit the ground like a rag doll. I thought you were dead or something, man. It was too cold, I had to bring you in the car."

I sat up, my head throbbing. "So, I didn't make the wish?"

He whipped his head around. "You better hope you didn't," he paused, then looked back into the headlight's beam and the two-lane highway which unraveled before us. "But if you think you did, you probably did," he mumbled.

"So, what?" I asked. "I didn't wish to be invisible like you did. I didn't screw it up."

"*I* didn't screw it up, either, Dan. He did. Or, it did."

"How?" I shot at him, a strange fear sprouting in my chest.

"Haven't you ever read The Monkey's Paw – or at least seen The Simpsons episode?"

"Yeah, I..."

"You can wish for whatever the hell you want, Dan, it won't come up the way it should. Not to mention your soul. It's gone. If you wished, he has it. And the world is a cold place when you don't have a soul."

"What do you mean?"

"Your body," he looked back at me, as if to check. "Soulless – there are *things* which will try to get in. You'll never sleep again."

"I don't believe in that stuff," I told him. "It's all..."

"You're lying to both of us right now. You've seen too much to be denying things."

I didn't admit it at the time – not even to myself – but V was right. I was in denial. I was attempting to shut out the immense fear building inside of me. And a spike of horror shot down my body as he pulled the car into my driveway, the headlights running across the dark windows of my house.

"No, no," I ducked down. "Not here. We need to go to my aunt's. MacDonald Street."

He pulled out – although a little too loudly – and started back down the street. I looked back at my house, grateful to see that it remained dark, then I climbed up into the passenger seat.

"Dude," I said to him. "What are you going to say? You can't just walk back into your house and tell the truth. Can you?"

"Sure I can," he said, though sort of as a question.

"They'll think you're nuts. You go missing for months and then suddenly return saying you got turned invisible after some demon deal? Think about it."

What do you want me to tell them?"

"I don't know. That you were kidnapped?"

"The truth is easiest, man."

"Okay, then everyone will know about the door."

He looked over at me, his eyes grave. He knew the consequences of that. "So what?" he tried.

"Everyone will..." I started, realizing that I already had everyone looking for the door. "They'll all go looking for it."

"Then so be it."

"Just leave out the part about the door."

He glanced at me, considering it.

We were close to my aunt's house, on one of my town's main roads, near the turn into her neighborhood. I happened to look over and see a police cruiser parked just off of the road. The officer sat in the driver's seat – the light of his computer screen upon his face – as he looked up from his notes and at our car.

Given my town's small size, anyone driving around at two in the morning immediately seemed a little suspicious. The only thing on our side was that the cops knew that the kids of our town had nothing better to do on a Friday night but drive around in their parent's cars to kill time.

But it was pretty late, even for that.

I tensed, holding my breath, looking back at where I had seen the cruiser. But only darkness filled the side mirror. One-hundred metres from the turn into my aunt's neighborhood, the emptiness of 2 a.m. filled the road we had just driven up. We were going to make it. But then my heart stopped. I saw a sudden flow of light. The cruiser started. It pulled from its spot and turned our way.

"Man, that cop is coming," I freaked. "If I get caught, I'm screwed. If I get caught with you, that's even worse."

V stared into the rear-view mirror. "Maybe they were just done doing what they were doing."

I watched in the side mirror. It was gaining on us, but not chasing us. The angry lights of a Dodge Charger got a few car lengths behind us, then steadied. I looked ahead, thinking maybe we were okay.

"V", I said. "The turn."

"Dammit," he said as we passed my aunt's road.

He hit the brakes, moved to pull a U-turn, then aborted, his eyes shooting up to the rear-view.

"It's fine, just take the next one," I said.

But it didn't matter. Blue and red lights flashed upon our mirrors. My heart hammered. I began to sweat.

"Do you even have your licence?" I asked as he pulled over.

He nodded, removing a wallet. We then made eye contact. He looked tired and just as scared as me. He'd been through a lot the last few months.

You'll never be able to sleep again.

"Leave out the door," I said.

He looked away from me and rolled down the window. The officer was just coming up the side, a flashlight in hand. Upon getting beside us, he immediately scanned our laps and the car console with the beam, then clicked it off.

"Just curious what two young guys are doing in the middle of the night driving a fifty-five-year-old woman's car?"

"It's my aunt's," I said.

"Can I see some IDs?"

This is when he really looked at our faces. He looked at mine, then looked at V's, and something on his face – lit by the streetlamps and the headlights of his cruiser – took pause. He stared at V as he took our cards. With the flashlight back on, he looked down at the licences in his hand.

"Mike Veller," he said, almost skeptically. He shone his light on V's face before asking: "Haven't you been missing for months?"

"Yes, sir," he said.

"Where did you..." he stuttered. "Where have you been?"

V glanced over to me, then back to the cop.

"Going missing on purpose is a horrible thing to do," the officer said. "Your parents were a mess. I remember seeing them at the station. Articles in the newspaper. Why didn't you tell them?"

"I just needed to get away," V blurted. "I'm sorry. I only meant for it to be a day or two, then it spiraled out of control."

The officer handed the IDs back. "Whatever. Get home and get to bed. Stop wasting your aunt's gas, Daniel."

He then walked back to his car, shaking his head in disgust.

"Thank you," I said to V once the window was back up. "But why *didn't* you tell your parents? I mean, you could have just written them a note or something, right?"

"It was hard for me to send messages. Like I said, I could only touch certain things at certain times. It seemed arbitrary. Plus, I couldn't face them. I never went to my house during that time."

"But you moved the stone for me."

"What stone?"

"To show me the key. When I went to your house."

"Why did you go to my house?"

"To look for clues. It's how I found you."

"Dan, I didn't move the rock," he said to me, his eyes wide and concerned. "It must have been him."

• • • •

I HAD A PLAN TO MEET up with Melissa on Saturday, and despite what had happened the previous night, it looked like the plan was still on.

I slept late since I was out late. V and I had dropped off my aunt's Acadia and went our separate ways. I'm sure it was an emotional night at the Veller's house. But because I had slept late, by the time Melissa and I planned to meet up, the sun was already going down. Mind you, this occurred in the middle of winter, so it was really only around 5 p.m.

I planned to come clean to Melissa about everything. It would be easier now that she knew the truth. She must have, if she were to sign her name. A part of me couldn't wait to reveal to her that I'd known all along. Another part of me hated that I hadn't told her earlier. Maybe she would have gone to the door with me instead. I could have stopped her from wishing, then stopped me from wishing.

But, she had gone with Allyster. Because she liked him more.

And I wished for her not to.

I didn't know for sure if it had worked, but she was the one who had texted me earlier in the day to remind me of our plan. She seemed eager. Her entire attitude had changed in just one day, so I took it as a sign.

I waited at my house for her. My parents had gone into the city for a work party, and my sister had gone out with friends. My house – a two-story in your average neighbourhood – stood still and quiet. I put some music on, but still a lonely presence loitered. So, I changed the music to the radio, as it made me feel more connected. Maybe it's because radio is live, and if the people on the radio are okay – wherever they are – maybe I am, too.

I waited in the living room. I wore nice clothes, my hair looked the best it could, and I felt nervous. I'm not sure if I was more nervous about the truth of everything that had happened, or that Melissa was about to walk into my house. But V had returned home, and as far as I was concerned, all of this stuff about the door could end. The nonsense about souls was insane, and I'm sure V would come to realize that delusion after winding down and settling back into normal life.

Regardless, I still felt the need to share it with Melissa. And as I pondered what had happened and what could have happened, I realized why. Melissa had made a wish. In the case that V was right about what our wishes had been traded for, her fate mirrored mine.

Headlights flashed across the front window. My heart picked up, but I took a breath and settled it back down. I looked through the curtains. The lights of the car shut off. It was Melissa in her Volvo. When she finally got to the door and I let her inside, I didn't refrain from that burning question.

"What did you wish for?" I asked her.

She looked at me, taken aback. "How did you know about the wish?"

"I know all about the door."

"I thought I had made the wish. I thought I had gone into the door," she spilled, gratefully. "But then Allyster said I didn't go anywhere at all. It was so strange," she stared at me with those eyes. There seemed to be something less about them now. "I started to believe Allyster, but then..." she looked at me, her face tense.

"Then what?"

"Then my wish came true."

PART ELEVEN

"What happened?" I asked her as she took off her boots and winter jacket.

She looked behind me, then into the living room.

"No one is home," I told her.

"Still," she said. "Can we go to your room? I want to see your room."

I nodded. "Sure."

I had cleaned my room just in case. I couldn't risk her seeing it in its usual state. I was grateful for that foresight as she closed the door and sat on my computer chair. I sat on the bed across from her. I looked at her with prying, albeit patient, eyes. She sighed, looking back at me with guilt ridden eyes.

"It's okay," I said.

She inhaled deeply. "I wasn't expecting to be asked to make a wish when I went inside the door," she started. "But a voice told me to. He said to write down my name on this wall and to make a wish. So, I did. I figured what was the harm? I felt stupid, but I just loudly said that I wished I was the lead in the play instead of Hannah."

"Then what happened?" I sat on the edge of the bed, wondering if she had seen V.

"I just heard Allyster repeating my name. Next thing I knew he was looking at me strangely, asking me if I was okay."

A gust of wind howled at the window. A pained expression came across her face and she looked at the glass and the blackness beyond it. "I got a call once we got back to Allyster's apartment. It was Hannah. She was so upset, and what if it was my fault?"

"If what was your fault?"

"Hannah said she had been skating on her cousin's pond and she somehow broke her leg. She said she fell, but she doesn't understand how it broke anything. Now she's in a cast and will be for two months. She won't be able to do the play at all."

"Could just be a coincidence," the words left my mouth. But I knew it wasn't.

"Then, after that," she ignored me, "I had been feeling strange since having left the door. But I felt strange in another way, too. I was with Allyster and everything he said started to bug me. Everything he did was annoying. I had to leave. I was upset about Hannah, and he tried to comfort me, but it just made me so mad."

"That's weird," I said, starting to feel guilty myself.

"I just wanted to talk to you about it. I like you, you like me. Screw Allyster."

"If you like me, then why were you ignoring me?"

"I don't know," she said. "I guess Allyster got into my head. He said you didn't actually like me, that you did this with all girls. He told me that I'm graduating soon and him and I didn't have long to be together and I couldn't waste it being in the middle of you two. But I realize now that he was wrong. He was just trying to play me. He's an asshole."

I cringed slightly, and guilt fought with my triumph of winning Melissa over. But did I really do it? Was it fair that I had influenced her decision?

It wasn't. But it was too late. She left the chair and sat beside me.

"Thanks for always listening," she said.

"Of course," I smiled.

She smiled back and gave me a kiss on the cheek.

"But," I said to her. "There's more."

She sat back and looked at me. I had planned to tell her the truth, but how could I tell her about my wish? I looked into her eyes as they waited for *more*.

"I knew about the door that first night we went looking for it," I told her. "Not all of it yet, but I knew that a friend of mine from work had gone missing because of it."

"Why didn't you tell us?"

"He had been missing a while. I didn't want to be a suspect or something. I don't know. I wanted to tell you the truth."

And I still did. I wanted to tell her about the souls and my negative wish. But if she had her soul again and I had her, did it really matter?

• • • •

THAT FOLLOWING MONDAY I had missed the bus, so I had no choice but to take the heel-toe express to school. It was a bit of a hike, and I'd either get to first period toward the end of class, or I'd miss it completely. I'd rather miss it if I were going to miss most of it anyway, so I took my time. I listened to music and enjoyed the light exercise. I had a lot to think about, anyway. Melissa and I had planned our first official date for next week. Dinner and a movie. Standard stuff. I was excited to buy flowers and open the car door for her. Even though she would be the one driving, I'd still do it.

It finally felt as though things could calm down. All of the madness with the door could be over. V was home and Melissa liked me. It seemed to be a win-win. It's not like I wished for her to like me. She liked me by her own voli-tion.

But, as much as I tried to ignore them, some aspects didn't add up.

V said that something else had helped me into his house, that something else had guided me to the door. It didn't make sense why it would do that. Clearly some entity wanted to lure people and had the ability to grant wishes in exchange for their souls. But V had said to reverse it you had to lure someone else there yourself and have them make a wish.

He also said that he had found keys to unlock the door and that someone named Kate had texted him. Was Kate out there somewhere, having escaped the door? Did all of those names belong to people out in the world just living their lives? Or were some of them kept?

Kept where?

I didn't know. But as I continued along the street – the same main street on which V and I had gotten pulled over – his red Cavalier squealed into an emp-ty parking lot in front of me. He looked frantic and scared behind the wheel as the car jerked to a stop. He busted open the door and looked at me.

"Dan?" he asked.

I looked around. "Yeah?"

"Get in," he said. "Just get in. Just you," he smacked the roof of the car. "Now!"

Maybe I shouldn't have listened to him, but I did anyway, and once inside, he peeled out of the parking lot, headed the way I had just come.

"What the hell are you doing, V?" I looked out the window. "Can you drive me to the school at least? I'm late."

"Listen, Daniel. You made a wish," he said, turning the car around. "I'm still being haunted. My soul. I don't have it. He keeps the souls *and* takes away your wish. I can't sleep. You're vulnerable when you sleep. They can get in. I think the longer you wait..." he shook his head, looking toward me.

My jaw hung open, my eyes gazing toward his madness. If this meant what I thought it meant, then not only did I not have my soul, but Melissa didn't have hers, either. And we could never get them back.

"Did your wish come true?" V asked, looking me up and down as though it would be obvious.

I nodded. "Yeah. It did."

"So you did make one. Then that's it. You may as well keep your wish, dude, because getting rid of it doesn't help. You won't get your soul back."

"Where is my soul?" I asked. "I still feel like I have it."

"You – look – you technically are still connected to your soul," he said. "I mean, I think. You must be. But the link is weak because it doesn't belong to you. It belongs to him. And when you die, your soul – you – goes to him."

My heart jumped at that. I began to panic. "But you said you never went to your house. That means it was helping me. Why would it help me if –"

"You choose someone. You start trying to get them to go. Then he helps them. If someone is actively looking for the door, he will help."

"Why do you keep saying *he*?"

V nodded, his eyes intent on the road. "I saw him."

I stared at him with curious eyes until he glanced over at my silence.

"He was made of fire. Smokeless fire," he paused. "That's the best I can describe it."

"How did you know it was him?"

"I knew," he said quietly. "You would too if you saw him."

There was silence. I would die one day and go to that fear, that sense of terror I had felt during sleep paralysis – that entity which held the candle behind the door. That presence will be what comes to collect me. It will take me somewhere filled with the shadows of evil beings.

Unless I could stop it.

"What do we do?"

"We get someone to help us," he answered.

"Like who?" I asked. "A priest?"

He chuckled as he pulled into the parking lot of my school. "No. This is elemental. This is a part of nature. Something that has always been here. We need to find someone experienced in the unseen world around us. We need to find a shaman."

"What?"

"Trust me on this. Look, you need to come with me. This concerns you just as much. Have the dreams started yet?"

"I don't think..."

"You're lucky. They're terrible. And," he looked out into the parking lot, terrified, "I think they're more than just dreams."

• • • •

I DIDN'T GO WITH V. Again, I left him on his own. And again, I paid for it.

When I walked into school, into the empty halls – period one still going – the weight of death hung over me. It wasn't something someone at my age generally worried about. But when this life ended, one of horrors awaited me. All because I wanted to get a girl to like me. And her soul, too, was forever *his*, because I got her involved.

"Dan," a voice said.

I turned around with a jump. Up a hall, having just come out of the washroom, was Allyster.

"Dude," he said. "Was wondering where you were this morning. Sleep in?"

I nodded, the world around me a buzz.

"Hey man, what's gotten into Melissa?" he asked, pulling out his phone. "She keeps sending me these angry texts saying she hates me and she hopes I die. It's really messed up. Should I tell someone about it? It just came out of nowhere."

"No, don't," I said. "I'll talk to her. Look, I'm sorry about everything that's happened."

He shrugged. "It's okay, man. It's nothing."

Through the halls, the bell rang. The closed, quiet doors which surrounded us suddenly burst open at once, people flooding around us.

"Oh, wow," I said. "I didn't realize that it was so late."

Before Allyster could respond, Eric and another guy named James – also in our friend group – came up to us.

"So, Allyster," Eric said. "Did you and Melissa really find the door?"

"Yeah," he said. "It was weird. Melissa like freaked out and she's hated me since."

"What a bitch," James said.

I inhaled to say something – not sure what – but Eric spoke first:

"We're going to try and find the door this weekend. We want to open it, unlike you, yah wuss."

"I told you, Melissa was just acting too weird, so we left."

"You guys shouldn't," I blurted.

They all looked at me.

"Don't go looking for the door," I said.

"Oh, the door, don't go," someone called as they passed us in the halls. It was a group of hockey players, all in Melissa's grade. One looked back at us as the rest of them laughed. "Or thee leprechauns, they'll follow yah home."

Eric and James turned to me. "Is it true? Will the leprechauns follow us home?"

"Dude," Allyster said. "I went to the door and I'm fine. It's just a dumb door. Hard to find though. I don't even remember how we got there to be honest…"

"I'll only say it once," I looked to them. "Don't go looking for the door. Just don't."

"That's actually the second time you've said it," James pointed out.

"Yeah," Allyster said. "And you've never even been to the door so what do you know?"

"Okay, look," Eric said. "If you don't want us to look for the door, we won't. But let's have a guy's night this weekend. No door. We'll just go see a movie or something. James just got his licence and we want to do *something*. We haven't all hung out in forever."

"Yeah, let's do that," I said. "Friday."

"Sounds good, guys," Allyster agreed.

• • • •

OUTSIDE THE WINDOWS, a dim blue sky grew dark above the cold dead maples. I had finished my homework and dinner. While we ate, my parents brought up the fact that V had come back. Thankfully, they didn't say much else about it. I mentioned my date with Melissa and my parents didn't object – my grounding unceremoniously lifted. But my dad did eye me, still thinking I had become something else – a criminal who had slipped under his radar. For I didn't know it at the time, but my father knew a little more than I thought he did.

I sat at my desk, ready to play some Warcraft before bed. Maybe an hour or two, depending on what I got up to. I needed the escape. The idea of sleep scared me as I worried about the dreams. I hoped that V only spewed nonsense, having lost the plot. Maybe he did. Maybe I still had my soul, Melissa didn't like Allyster for other reasons, and it was all just a coincidence. Maybe V really did lose his mind after going missing for so long. I could only hope. Because as I fired up Warcraft, reached into a fresh bag of potato chips, and looked down at my phone with a new text from Melissa, I thought that things couldn't be better.

If I forgot about the door, maybe it would forget about me, too.

• • • •

I WALKED TOWARD THE door. They followed behind me. I turned to look at them. The terrified faces of Allyster, Eric, and James looked back at me. No, they looked past me. As I realized this, I heard the creaking of a door hinge. I turned forward to see the door fully open. In the dark, he stood. A humanoid form which vanished downward into the wispy tail of a ghost. It floated, made of fire. It was like V had said – smokeless fire. But another thing. The fire emitted no light. Despite the flames which raged from his body, despite the fact that he himself appeared bright, the door and trees around him kept dark.

The being's eyes burned denser. A grin which revealed blackness began to spread across its face. I stepped back to join my friends in the horror, but they were gone. James' mom's RAV4 had vanished. It was only forest behind me. Before me, the being raised a strong fiery arm and beckoned me into the darkness behind it.

Bzzt.

It laughed noiselessly.

Bzzt.

I woke up, my chest heaving, my face sweaty.

Bzzt.

My phone. A call. Allyster. I picked it up, still panting.

"Hello?"

"Dan," a voice said. A female voice.

"Who is this?"

But by the time I had asked, I knew.

"Melissa?"

"You need to come to Allyster's. Don't tell anyone you're coming. I only meant to scare him, but..."

"But what?" I asked, the world spinning around me.

"He's dead."

He had grinned because he knew. He knew that at that moment, as I slept, Melissa was murdering Allyster.

I'd told her I was coming. I told her without hesitation and I don't know why. But after hanging up I dialed 9-1-1. I looked at the number on my phone screen for a long time, my thumb hovering above the green button. Melissa would go to jail. For murder. But she *did* murder somebody.

Because of me.

It was my fault and I knew it. But I could fix it too. A plan sprouted in my mind, and it seemed the easiest. Foolproof. So, I put down my phone and quietly got dressed, wondering deep down if I could really do what I got ready to go do. It was just after two in the morning and outside of my window things were frigid and haunting. The moon shone brightly down onto the skeletal trees, casting their twisted shadows lightly upon the layer of snow which covered my backyard.

I stared out at it. Had the call been a part of the nightmare? Was it a dumb joke? Could I just go back to bed and peacefully fall asleep?

Though I wished I could answer yes to those questions, I knew the answer was no. So, I layered up and prepared for an awful bike ride. I crept down the stairs with pajama pants beneath my jeans, two pairs of socks, and two long-sleeved shirts below my hoodie. I slipped my jacket on as quiet as ever and grabbed my gloves.

"Where are you going?"

I spun toward the living room, a slight cry leaving my throat. From the darkness I could see the light of my sister's phone upon her face. She sat on the couch.

"What the hell are you doing?" I asked.

"I'm texting my friend who just broke up with his girlfriend. What are *you* doing?"

My pounding heart fluttered. I felt trapped beneath the layers of my clothes, suddenly hot and sweaty. My potential girlfriend murdered one of my best friends and I had to go help hide the body. But of course, I couldn't tell my sister. She was already going to spill this encounter to Mom and Dad.

"Same," I said. "But I'm biking to her house."

"Melissa?"

"What?" I shot. "So what if it is?"

"Easy," she mumbled, looking back at her phone. "Everyone knows you're hopelessly in love with her."

"No they don't," I looked at her. But she was busy texting. "Whatever. Don't tell Mom and Dad you saw me leave."

She didn't answer. My phone vibrated.

Melissa> *Dan. Are you coming? I'm scared.*

Dan> *Leaving now.*

• • • •

I SHOOK THE WHOLE RIDE over and I wasn't sure if it was because of the cold or the reality of what I biked toward. Although I felt as though I could fix it, I still wanted to do anything else but see.

And what If I couldn't fix it?

As I rode up to Allyster's apartment I saw her car on the side of the road out front. I braked, stopping beside it. I sat astride on my bike and looked up at the window. The curtains were drawn. A light shone dimly behind them. My hope that this was some sort of messed up prank remained. I truly hoped so. But if not, my last chance to call the police without being too involved sat in that moment.

Looking up at the window, I noticed a tall dark figure – darker than the darkness around it. The man wore a wide-brimmed hat and peered out at me from the window above Allyster's. But just as I noticed him and shot my eyes upward, the shape carried away into the shadows. A sickness came about me and I pulled out my phone, texting Melissa that she needed to come down and let me in.

I waited there, on my bike, praying she'd never come. It was hardly fifteen seconds – not even ten – but it felt like I had waited all night when I finally heard a sound from the other side of the foyer door.

Through the glass, I watched in horror as she cautiously walked down each step, one by one. Blood covered her sweater, her hands, and even parts of her face. I stood astride on my bike on the side of the empty road. It was moonlit, quiet, and dreadfully cold. But still, I sweat bullets.

I got off my bike, leaned it against the front of his building, and exhaled deeply. My breath burst out around me in the light above his building door. I opened it as she opened the one on the other side of the foyer. She looked at me just as fearfully as I did at her. Tears rushed my eyes. I did this to her. It was my fault.

"I'm going to fix it," I told her, though it came out as a sob. "I promise. You might not realize when I do, but it will be fixed."

She shushed me. "Hurry," she started up the stairs. "Before someone sees us."

Once at the top of the stairs, she motioned for me to turn the corner and go first. I did. The door to Allyster's apartment stood open.

Allyster's apartment seemed quiet and normal. It smelt the same. Felt the same. Then the normality cracked as I walked farther inside. A shelf in the living room beside the couch – the couch which Allyster actually slept on, since the apartment was only a one bedroom – had fallen forward, leaning against the table beside it. Everything which had once been on that shelf now covered the floor and couch. A deodorant stick, cologne, a watch – a bunch of random things that would typically be in someone's bedroom.

I walked a few more steps and the normality was torn away completely. The coffee table was pushed forward to make room for Allyster's body. Blood soaked into the rug which lay beneath him. On the hardwood beside the rug was a deep red puddle. Allyster lay on his back, his entire front side full of stab wounds.

I stared at the scene in horror. My stomach turned. I couldn't move. I didn't want to. I wanted Allyster to move – to get up and laugh and say *gotcha*.

But it was all too real.

The door shut behind me. And suddenly I felt sick for a different reason. I was alone with a murderer. I turned to Melissa. I looked down at her hands.

"Where's the knife?" I asked.

She raised her hand. I stepped back. But she merely pointed. I turned and looked. I must have missed it, for the small blade sat on the floor about a foot away from him.

"He deserved it," she said.

I shot her a look, but her face appeared twisted and sad.

"We need to clean this up," I told her.

She nodded, then stepped forth. "Wait," she grabbed my arm. "Shouldn't we call the cops. I killed someone, Dan."

I looked her in the eyes. They were watery, now missing the same thing I was missing.

A soul.

Her face was close to mine. I could smell her perfume – a smell I had come to love. I tended to hate perfumes, but something soft emanated from hers. With our eyes deep into each other's, we leaned closer together. We kissed. We french kissed. I put my hand up and touched her face as we kissed some more. She was perfect. And she wouldn't be going to prison.

Whether she decided to hate me or not, I needed to tell her the truth. I pulled back from our kiss, the body of our friend still laying behind me.

"Look," I said. "You can hate me if you want, but I need to tell you something. It's how we're going to fix this, okay?"

She nodded, her eyes intense.

"I went to the door. I made a wish," I paused. "I wished for you to hate Allyster."

"What?" she sobbed. "You did this to me?"

"I just..."

"I've been going insane," she yelled. "I haven't been able to concentrate on anything. Or sleep. I've just been obsessed with how anyone could let Allyster continue to go on living his life when he was just so... so... I don't even know!"

"Stop yelling," I said. "Look, all we need to do to fix this is to get someone else to find the door and wish for this to have never happened."

She stared at me, still pissed, but understanding the plan.

"Until then," I continued, "we need to cover this up the best we can."

• • • •

WE PUT TOWELS OVER Allyster's abdomen, wrapped him in the rug, and taped it shut. After cleaning up the blood and rearranging everything to look as normal as possible, I turned to Melissa.

"Bring your car around the back of the building," I said.

She nodded, grabbed her purse, and left. I stood in the apartment alone, looking down at the rolled up rug which concealed my dead friend.

"I'm sorry," I croaked. "I'm going to fix it."

And I wondered if I could.

Could a wish be too powerful?

I grabbed an end of the rug and pulled it toward the door. It was heavy and bulky, but it had to be done. Once I got him into the hallway – praying the other tenants were fast asleep – I grabbed Allyster's keys from the key ring, turned out the lights to his apartment, then shut and locked the door.

• • • •

MELISSA AND I HAD GOTTEN the rug – the body – into her car without any trouble or sign of witnesses. We drove east, into the country. To us, it didn't matter where we dropped the body, because it wouldn't be a body for long.

The car ride was unlike any of the others we'd had. No music played and no funny stories were told. The dread of what we had done and had gotten involved with hung over us.

Eventually, we found an unmaintained road which ran alongside a steep hill, overlooking the many shadows of thick woods. Melissa stopped the car and popped the trunk. Her headlights shone off into the dead trees which hung over the trail. Her taillights cast dimly onto the frozen dirt behind. Our shadows obstructed this as we lifted the trunk and pulled out the rug.

Without a word, we brought it over to the hill, swung it three times, and released it downward. With a ruckus of cracks and snaps, the rug hit the foliage and rolled farther below, out of our site. In the night, it appeared to be gone and hidden for good.

"Soon, it will be like it never happened," I promised her.

She said nothing and returned to the car. I followed, getting in the passenger seat. After a moment of silence, she finally spoke:

"Should we go looking for the door now?" she turned to me. "To make the wish?"

I shook my head. "I don't think we can wish twice," I told her. "It'll have to be someone else. Someone who hasn't wished before."

She stared at me, her eyes unsure.

"I did this to you. I'll take care of it."

She leaned in, kissed me, and again it was incredible. As we kissed, as she crawled over the console – from her seat to mine – in the warmth of her Volvo and her lovely perfume, someone else who would now have to be dragged into the horror of the door slept soundly.

PART THIRTEEN

O n Tuesday morning, Melissa got called to the drama room in first period and learned that she could have the lead role if she wanted it, and that her original role would be given to someone else. But – she was warned – the play debuted that weekend and she would have to learn all of her new lines in that time.

She took the part.

I stood in the hall by my locker, texting her congratulations – tired, scared, and excited by all that had happened the night before.

"Dude," James nudged me. "Seen Allyster?"

I turned to see him and Eric. "No," I said. "Maybe he's sick?"

"You know that guy would come to school even if he was dying."

I shrugged. "I don't know. But listen, we should go look for the door on Friday. I was being dumb before. Let's just do it."

"Sweet," Eric said.

"Glad to see you've grown a pair of balls," James said.

"Yeah, we'll see who has the balls when we find the door."

Eric shook his head. "I'll pass on that last part."

"You know what I meant," I said. "Come on, let's head to second period."

• • • •

I HAD MADE THE LAST wish. I was the one to get people to go. I had to choose someone, get them interested in the door, and *he* would guide them. And that is why – come Wednesday night – I hid behind the back seat of James' parent's SUV. I had waited around the side of his house, shivering from the cold – a tall shadow in the night. I prayed he would pick up what I had put down and head to the door without me and Eric.

Gratefully, he did. He came out, unlocked the car, and that's when I gently swooped in through the rear door. By the time he sat down, buckled his seatbelt, and pressed the start button, I was hidden away.

See, I couldn't wait until Friday to find the door with the guys. Things had gotten too out of hand. The wish had to be made as soon as possible. And it was going to be made by James.

• • • •

BY NOON ON WEDNESDAY, normality had vanished. Allyster had been announced missing that morning. But before that could explode in my face, something else did.

"Do you think he ran away?" Eric asked as we sat down for lunch. "I mean, he can be an emotional guy sometimes. But he seemed fine last time I saw him," he turned to me. "A little pissed at you though."

"For what?" I asked.

"Uh," he looked to James. "Melissa. Duh."

"I didn't do anything."

"You took his girl."

"No I didn't. She was never his girl. We were all friends and she chose me."

"Whatever," James said. "But you've got to admit she's gotten in the middle of you two."

"Maybe she did," I said, feeling my phone vibrate in my pocket – surely another text from Melissa.

But I didn't care if she had gotten in the middle of Allyster and I. We were going to fix our mistake. It would be like Allyster had never vanished – *died* – at all, and then her and I could forget all of this stuff.

Well, almost all of it.

"Daniel," a cry blared across the cafeteria.

The cafeteria was a good size, and at lunch time it filled up quite a bit – currently packed to the brim. The school split lunch periods, so basically half of the school was in there eating lunch. Because the tables folded into benches, it also doubled as our auditorium, the same room in which I would soon be co-starring in a play. A giant wall of windows which looked out at the winter landscape of our school's football field stretched along the exterior side. The entrance from the foyer covered the wall opposite. Standing in this entrance – in one of the many doorways – was Mike Veller. His hair looked like he had just lifted it off a pillow. His clothes were torn and his nose had dried blood beneath it.

He called my name again, making the whole room go from quiet to completely silent. The whole world collapsed in on me as every pair of eyes in that room slowly found me.

"Daniel," he cried again once *his* eyes found me. He began toward me – more of a stumble than a walk.

"V," I said in the horrible stillness of over a hundred people. "What are you doing?"

"He's coming," he said. "It won't be tonight, but he – when it happens, it won't be easy."

"Come on," I said to him, starting toward the doors. "Let's talk outside."

"Don't go looking for the door," he screamed to everyone.

"Oh," someone squealed. "Or thee leprechauns."

To be fair – something I may have left out – V's hair was red.

"What is going on here?" the principal – Mr. Glad – stepped through the door V had just come in a second ago. His voice boomed across the large room.

"Nothing," I said. "We were just going outside."

"Daniel," Mike – despite the social massacre he'd just committed upon my life – continued. "Your wish. What did you wish for? It'll turn it against you."

"V," I snapped. "Stop."

"You said it came true."

"Both of you in my office," Mr. Glad demanded.

I started toward the doors, grabbing V along the way. But he grabbed me back, spun me, and looked into my eyes. His were bloodshot, tired, and scared. No – *petrified*.

"I went north," he said before half of my school, though quietly. "Far north. The shaman. I told him what happened."

I stared at him, my eyes stern. "And?"

He chuckled. "There's no going back from any of it. We go to him," he nodded with a crazed grin. "And he decides when."

• • • •

"YOU DIDN'T GO TO THIS school, did you, Mr. Veller?" Mr. Glad asked, his eyes on his computer.

We both sat in his office, facing the principal who sat at his desk.

"No," V answered.

"Okay," Mr. Glad sighed. "How do you two know each other?"

"We both work at No Frills," I said.

Mr. Glad nodded. "And what happened to your face?" he looked to Mike.

I, too, looked to Mike. He glanced at me, and I glared with eyes which begged him to relent. But alas...

"Sir, I made a mistake. I went missing over the fall and Christmas..."

"That was you?"

V nodded. "See, north of town there's this door."

"Oh, I've heard of this," Mr. Glad grumbled.

"Really?" I asked.

"Yep. My daughters went out looking for it the other night."

V's eyes doubled in size. "You can't let them. They can't. That's where I went," he stood up, now yelling. "*I found the door. That's where I was!*"

"You need to sit down," Mr. Glad hollered.

His voice startled us both.

"V," I said. "Please, you need to chill."

V sunk slowly into his seat. "Easy for you to say," he said. "You haven't seen the worst of it yet. You haven't –"

"I saw him," I cut him off quietly. "Smokeless fire, like you said."

"You did..." V breathed.

"What the hell are you talking about?" Mr. Glad frowned.

"Look," I said. "He's not lying. Something weird is up with that door. There's a... demon. It grants a wish, but it doesn't work out how it should."

"A wish?" he asked, somewhere in the middle of condescending and curious.

I nodded.

"And you say this being looks like smokeless fire?"

"Yeah," I said.

He stared at the desk for a moment. It was a long moment in the silence of the room, the blatancy of people walking by the office and trying to nonchalantly look in pressing upon me. But they became easier to forget once Mr. Glad continued:

"I used to teach world religion. Actually was my minor in university. Now, I'm not saying that I believe any of this crap. But what you're describing sounds a bit like the djinn."

"What is that?" V said, on the edge of his seat.

"Think of it as a demon from hadith scripture."

"Hadith?"

"Islam," he explained. "A spirit of sorts that, well," he sighed, agitated.

"What?"

"This is all just a bunch of..." he rolled his eyes. "The fact that I'm entertaining your friend's story here. But look, it's said that the djinn – though from their own realm – is everywhere and sometimes someone can summon one to do their bidding."

V turned to me. "Then who is controlling it, Dan?"

Mr. Glad sighed again, hating himself for this conversation. "Look, if we're willing to accept the existence of the djinn, then there's an array of subsequent truths."

"Such as?" I asked.

"Come on," he said. "Think about it. If this spirit from another dimension exists, then that other dimension – and all which it contains or could contain – must exist."

I looked to V. "What if..." I said to him. "I mean it wants our souls..."

"Oh, give me a break," Mr. Glad murmured.

But I ignored him, my eyes still on V's. "What if it's working with something from somewhere else?"

"Somewhere else..." V repeated.

"Another dimension."

• • • •

"DUDE," JAMES ASKED. "*What* the hell was that?"

I walked through the hall with him and Eric, pulling half a dozen eyes my way with each step.

"I don't want to talk about it, dude," I said. "He's just a little – unwell."

"You think?" Eric asked.

"Dude, you've officially got the entire school wanting to find that door. Even the hockey players were talking about going."

I shook my head. "Fine," I said. "But don't let anyone say that I didn't warn them. That V didn't warn them."

• • • •

V HAD LEFT – ON A NEW mission. I skipped my last two classes. Melissa skipped with me. We sat in her car in the parking lot.

"He said that in front of everyone?" she asked, her hands in front of the heater.

I nodded. "Now everyone wants to find the door."

"How do we stop them?"

"I don't know," I said. "But I need to get there first with James and Eric so that one of them can wish for Allyster to be alive again."

"At least I want that, too," she said. "I don't feel the hate I did before for him. It stopped last night, I think. Before that, a part of me wanted him to stay dead."

"Wait," I said. "So, my wish is no longer true, then. That means someone else must have found the door," I turned to her. "Someone else made a wish."

"I thought you said that your friend said that the wishes don't go away. That they turn against you."

I shrugged. "I don't know what to believe about what he says. I mean, he says that, but he's not invisible anymore, right? He also said that he – whatever is behind the door – tried to come get him."

She looked at me, terrified.

"We can fix it," I said. "We just have to start with Allyster."

• • • •

I NEEDED A PLAN. SURE, I wanted to find the door, but so did everyone else. What if they found it at the same time as me? What if they all wished for things which ruined them? With an array of questions whirling around me as I walked home from my bus stop, I turned the corner onto my street and realized that – questions or no questions – I had to send someone to the door to make the wish.

And it had to be that night.

Two police cruisers sat outside of my parent's house. As I walked closer, I debated fleeing. But there was nowhere to go. Plus, fleeing would make me look guilty as hell if they didn't already think I was.

Walking down the cold sidewalk – the odd car passing by, the drivers warm behind the wheel – I pulled out my phone. I went to my text conversation with

Melissa. I wanted to warn her. To ask if police were at her house, too. Instead, I typed something else:

Dan> *Delete the text where I asked you to come downstairs. Then delete this one. Now.*

With a huge oversight, I took a deep breath, turned up my driveway, and walked into my house. In the living room waited both of my parents, my sister, and two officers. I instantly recognized one of them as the officer who pulled V and I over.

"Dan," my mom said. "Can we talk to you?"

I nodded slowly and sat down.

"We just have a few questions," the officer who had pulled us over – while eyeing me as though he'd cracked the case – said.

"Why was your bike at Allyster's apartment?" the other cop asked. She, too, seemed confident that the deal had been sealed.

"I go there all the time," I stuttered. "I just left it there a few days ago when I was offered a ride home instead."

She nodded, writing on a pad.

"Did you go anywhere on Monday night, early Tuesday morning?"

I glanced to my sister. We locked eye contact, then she looked away.

"No," I said.

"We need you to understand the severity of the situation here," she said.

I nodded. I looked to my mom. Her eyes were watering. My dad stood with his arms crossed, his eyes concentrated on the floor.

"Allyster's body was found earlier today," the officer continued. "He was stabbed to death."

"Okay," I said, my eyes also watering.

"Do you know *anything* about that?"

I shook my head, unable to utter a word as I cried, the reality of it smashing into me.

The male officer reached into a case. He removed a Ziploc bag which contained Allyster's cell phone – the same phone as mine.

We had gotten them together.

"Can you explain, then, why he made an eighteen second phone call to you right around the time of his death?"

PART FOURTEEN

The Ziploc bag with the phone sat on the coffee table and while I sat and cried and everyone gave me a moment, I – with some strange bout of courage – turned off my phone and swapped it with Allyster's. Like the motivation to walk up V's driveway, the action seemed to come from elsewhere – a motion made by me, but commanded by something else.

"Son," the male officer came back into the room. "We're not saying you're responsible. But if you know anything – even the slightest thing – about what might have happened to your friend, we need to know."

I shook my head. "That call was just a pocket dial. I picked it up and went back to sleep. I didn't hear anything on it."

He eyed me. "We found two sets of fingerprints both on Allyster's body and in his apartment. We have taken and run these prints with no match."

Everyone else now gathered back into the living room.

"We need to take a sample of your fingerprints to clear your name," the officer continued. "My partner and I can do it here or we can do it down at the station. Your choice."

I looked to my family behind the officer. I looked at my sister. But she wouldn't look up from the floor. I nodded to the female officer who held a small case.

"I'll do it here," I said.

They were going to take my fingerprints, run them for analysis, then find that they matched one of the sets of fingerprints involving Allyster's death. It would be sometime before bed, or maybe first thing in the morning, that I would be arrested, then questioned on who the other person was.

Then tried for murder.

They took my prints. They took the bag with my phone in it. Then they left. As the door shut, a discomfort filled the house like a gas.

"I know about last week," my dad spoke first. "You were pulled over in Aunt Pam's car with Mike Veller the night he returned home."

"Okay," I said, wishing I was out in the woods and with the door so I could wish this sick nightmare away.

"Okay?" he spat. "Where the hell was he? Were you keeping him somewhere?"

"What? No," I snapped. "Are you insane? He went missing in the woods and I found him with the GPS after remembering something he'd told me at work *months* ago."

The lie came out of my mouth, unplanned, but pretty good, I'd say.

"Where in the woods?" my mom frowned.

"Just... like, an abandoned cabin," I said, digging myself deeper.

My parents looked to each other.

"You said you were going to Melissa's," my sister said.

"What?" my mom looked at her.

"Susan," I freaked. "What the hell?"

"You killed someone," she screamed.

"No, I didn't," I said. "I promise you guys."

She shook her head. "You left that night. On your bike. You said you were going to Melissa's, but when I looked out the window, you biked south. Melissa lives north. Allyster lives south."

My parents stared, mouths agape, unsure of what to do about their son being a murderer. Standing in the foyer, still by the door where we had seen the officers out, I began to slip on my shoes.

"I'm fixing all of it," I said to them. "Right now."

"You're not going anywhere," my mom yelled.

But before her, my dad, or my sister could step forward and stop me, I grabbed my jacket off of the hook and ran into the street, the sun already nearly set.

As I ran, I took out Allyster's phone, turned it on, and sent a text.

• • • •

Allyster> *If you want to find me, you have to find the door. Right now.*

IT WAS A LONG RUN TO James' house – the only one of our friends so far with his G2 – but I sent him the text and made it in time, waiting in the shadows until I could follow him into his parent's car.

He drove north. Good start. I pulled out Allyster's phone and texted him again. I heard it vibrate in his cup holder. On an empty country road, he slowed down to read it.

Allyster> *Keep going. You're almost there.*

"What the...?" he said aloud.
The car slowed down more-so as he replied:

James> *I have no idea where to go.*

Allyster> *Just go farther. Into the woods.*

The car accelerated again – though with uncertainty – down the road surrounded by trees. I didn't know where to go, either, but I did know that if he went far out enough, and if he wanted to find it bad enough, he would.
And I was right.

• • • •

I BELIEVE THE WORLD – the reality in which we live – has the ability to understand your desires and give them to you. Well, in a way. Like he who waits behind the door and hears your wish, there's a catch. While you may constantly think about how you don't want pickles on your burger or rain on a Saturday, like a search browser, the universe only hears the keywords. *Rain. Saturday.*
Thus, it gives you rain. On Saturday.
The door – as I would come to learn in such an atrocious way – operates similarly. The forces behind it – that which controls the wish granter – only heard the word *invisible* for V. Only heard *hate* for me. Only heard *lead of the play* for Melissa. And when V burst into my school and said that the wishes stay, but in another way, it was all of this that he meant.

Allyster> *Stop the car.*

On a skinny country road with dead winter limbs stretched over it, James read the text and did indeed bring the car to a stop.

James> *I'm not there yet. I don't know where to go. This is crazy. Can I just call you?*

I peeked over the back seat. James' head angled down toward his phone, likely waiting for my response. I ducked back down – a shrill wind bursting past the car – and texted him back, hoping that it would work.

Allyster> *Look up.*

There was a pause, followed by a subtle gasp. Then:
"What the hell," he said.

James> *Okay... I'm here.*

Allyster> *Get out of the car and walk toward the door.*

He sighed. He shut the car off.
"Oh, man," he whispered.
He waited another moment, the cold already creeping back into the RAV4. Then he opened his door and stepped into the snow. As he did, I opened the rear hatch, slid out, and walked up the driver's side of the car. He was facing the scene I had found on my bike, and again in the Acadia.
The door looked knowingly back at me as I crept up on my friend.
"James," I said.
He screamed, spinning toward me. "What the hell, dude?"
"Sorry."
"What are you doing here?"
"Listen to me," I said. "You need to do something really important."
He glanced back at the door, then at me – his eyes round and fearful in the moonlight.
"Okay?" I asked.
"What is it?"
"Go through the door..."
"No," he said. "Screw that," he reached for the car door.
"James, Allyster is dead," I blurted.
"What?"

"I have his phone. I was the one texting you."

"Why do you think he's dead?"

"He is," I stepped toward him. "And to bring him back, you have to go in through that door and wish that Allyster was never murdered. Those exact words."

"That's it?"

"That's it," I said. "Make the wish, write your name on the wall, then that's it."

He stared at me with flustered wonder, then – hesitantly – turned and slowly began toward the door. With sorry eyes, I watched him go.

"Dan," he called back at me, just a mere foot away from it. "Who killed him?"

I looked at the back of my friend, the moonlight reflecting off of the snow around us. He was a moment away from giving up his soul to save Allyster's life. With all of the guilt which weighed heavily upon me, I told him the truth.

"Melissa."

He stood for a moment, nodded, then opened the door and stepped through. It whacked shut with a warm gust of wind.

I stood and watched in the silence, unsure of *what* to watch. I couldn't hear him anymore. In fact, the only thing I did hear was a soft repetitive ping, like a jingle, which came from all around. As I looked into the sky – dark and gray – it grew louder. The alarm rang from every direction, then just one. A fierce light broke open the sky.

I woke up. I lay in my bed – cozy, not wanting to get up – as my arm reached out instinctively and hit snooze. I turned over and prepared to fall back asleep for five more precious minutes, but then I realized. Like a dream, the memory of being at the door with James – the police interrogation for Allyster's murder – rushed me.

I opened my eyes and sat up. My room was the same, but different. Subtly so. An open bag of potato chips sat on my computer desk, but I hadn't had chips in days. Not since...

I looked at my phone. It was Tuesday. The Tuesday after the night Melissa had killed Allyster.

But was it just a dream?

With the memory fully restored, it felt as real as sitting in my bed did. But clearly, it wasn't. Or, not anymore.

There was a text on my phone from Melissa, sent just a few minutes ago.

Melissa> *Want a ride to school? I can pick you up at like 8:10.*

Dan> *Sure!*

I put my phone down. The wish had worked.
But in the strangest way.
I picked my phone back up and texted Allyster.

Dan> *Hey man. What's up.*

Allyster> *Just got up. You?*

Filled with relief, I put my phone down again, got up, and began getting ready for school. I had fixed it. James had fixed it. And no one remembered a thing.

Despite this, things were far from over.

I don't expect you to believe what comes next.

PART FIFTEEN

Whatever the phenomenon is, it's intelligent. I believe that has been demonstrated already. To it, this is all a game. And it can't be beat. The last move always belongs to it.

Unless I can successfully release the truth.

"I had a weird dream last night," Melissa said as we pulled out of the Tim Horton's drive-thru and headed for school.

"What was it?" I asked.

She looked over at me as though she had a tinge of regret. But then she finally looked forward, back at the road. "I had a dream we kissed."

"Oh," I said, relieved. "Well, dreams come true sometimes, you know."

"Shut up," she chuckled.

Melissa dropped me off. She went to her class and I went to mine. It was science class. As I entered, I dreaded the prying eyes which would greet me after Mike Veller had caused a scene on my account in the cafeteria.

"You're late," Mr. Crowley said as I came in. "Oh, and you brought me coffee," he took the cup from me.

"It's actually a hot chocolate," I said.

He looked down at it – the entire class looking at us – and then handed it back to me, jerking his head toward my seat. The class chuckled as I sat down. But not at me. For some reason, it took me until that moment to realize that V hadn't come into the cafeteria to torment me. Not yet, anyway.

Relieved, I looked over at Allyster. He stared ahead at the teacher. I gave a small wave, trying to steal his attention – him only being three rows down – but he didn't look. Either way, it was amazing to see him there, alive and well.

"Now, there are several types of energy," Mr. Crowley said to the class. "There's atomic energy. This is the process of splitting atoms. It's called nuclear fission. An incredible amount of energy is released when this happens, which is why it is used in exotic systems, such as the atomic bomb," he looked over the class gravely. "However, there are lighter types of energy, like radiant energy," he grinned, holding back a chuckle. "Alright, it would be more funny had you already known what radiant energy is. Radiant energy is a combination of heat and light energy. Like a lightbulb or a campfire in the woods. The light travels outward in waves, casting onto all that is around it."

• • • •

"WHY DIDN'T YOU TEXT me back this morning, dude?" Allyster asked as we walked out of class.

"Uh," I said. "Sorry, I forgot."

"Yeah," he looked down at my Timmies cup. "Not because you were with Melissa, eh?"

"No, look..." I started.

"I had the weirdest dream," he shook his head, suddenly not caring.

"Last night?"

He nodded. "I still can't shake it. It felt so real. And, honestly," his voice lowered to a hush. "I don't even remember what happened last night."

"What do you mean?"

He stopped, his eyes solemn and scared, despite the liveliness around us. "It was late. I had ordered myself a pizza – you know, my dad isn't home for a bit – and the delivery guy had just left. I brought the pizza into the kitchen..."

I nodded.

"Well, this is where things get weird," he inhaled. "Melissa came over."

"She did?"

"Just listen. She knocks on my door out of nowhere. I answered and she comes in. Everything seems kind of normal, but she's acting weird. Like, there was just something in her eyes. I don't know how to describe it. Then, she kissed me."

"What?" I said, maybe a little too loud.

"But there was a pain in my torso. A deep one. I looked and she had stabbed me. She then started yelling at me about how I deserve this as she stabbed me again, and again. It was so painful and horrifying. I fought to get the knife from her, but the pain was too much. I died," he said. "Or, I thought I did. I woke up a few minutes before you had texted me. There was no sign she had been there. My pizza was sitting on the kitchen table, cold and untouched. I have no idea when I went to my bed and fell asleep."

I stared at him, trying to find the words to cover myself, not realizing that – for all anyone knew – I had no hand in the strange dreams of others.

"Hey, guys."

We jumped and turned. Eric put his arms around both of our shoulders.

"What's up? You guys excited to have a guy's night at my place Friday?"

"I thought James was going to drive us to the movies or something?" I asked.

Eric smiled curiously. "Who's James?"

"Look, guys," Allyster said. "I've got to go. We can talk more about Friday at lunch."

"James," I said to Eric as Allyster walked away. "Our friend, James?"

Eric frowned and shook his head. "You mean the kid in tenth grade who asked out Fiona Banks during his spot at the talent show?"

"No, I..." my heart began to pound. Suddenly the hall was hot and I felt I could throw up any second. "Never mind," I hurried off to the washroom.

The bathroom door closed behind me. A slight knock echoed against its vacant walls. I tossed the rest of my hot chocolate into the garbage and burst into one of the stalls. Bending over the toilet, I panted, my mind racing. Was James really gone? Had I... *erased him from existence?*

Gratefully, I didn't throw up. I stood, wiped the sweat from my forehead, and when I lowered my arm, the bathroom stood dark. The lights had gone out.

I stumbled through the darkness of the bathroom, toward the light which came from beneath the door. What I needed was a drink of water from the fountain. On a thin line cast upon the floor, I could see the wavering shadows of students walking by on the other side. I grabbed the handle and stepped into the hall, hoping Eric had left. But when my foot hit the hallway floor, it fell into a foot of snow. The bathroom door pulled shut, pushing me out. A trail before me led through the woods. Naked trees stood around it, their branches a tangle above. It was night and it was cold.

"Oh my God," I muttered.

I turned around to the bathroom door, but it wasn't the bathroom door. You can guess which door had replaced it.

"No," I yelled. "How?"

"Dan?"

I spun around. James – with his parent's Toyota RAV4 facing away from the door, its taillights bright against the snow and the exhaust flowing up from its tailpipe – stared at me with wide eyes.

"I was wondering where you went," he said. "I made the wish. Let's get the hell out of here."

He signalled with his head toward the SUV. Feeling sick once again, I started toward him. The RAV4's headlights shone down the path, into the woods and toward – hopefully – a road that would get us back into town.

"The headlights," a voice came from beside me. "Radiant energy."

I stopped, nearly colliding with Mr. Crowley. He nodded reassuringly, his eyes on the car. "The light travels in waves, outward and onto the surrounding woods, reflecting light off of them, allowing you to *see*."

"Uh, okay," I mumbled.

"But that light there," he pointed to the left, into the trees. "Does not travel out in waves."

I saw what he saw, and it was something I had seen before. It was the figure of a person, their body made of a fire which emitted no smoke and no light onto that which surrounded it.

"Why...?" I stuttered as the figure drew closer.

"Because, Dan," the teacher answered. "They're atoms not from our world. The energy required for them – for him – to be here with us right now? To have the so-called atoms of his world clashing with ours?" He shook his head in awe. "Tremendous."

"Dan, what are you doing?" James called. "Let's go."

"Don't you see him?" I asked.

Mr. Crowley vanished – likely never there at all – but the being in the woods still watched me. It advanced, and as it did, there was what could only be described as a dark grin spread across its face.

"How can you not see him?" I called, watching as the being continued to approach. "James?"

I looked back to the trail, but James and the SUV were gone as well. And when I looked back toward the woods, the entity loomed before me. The fire of him seemed bright, but the forest remained dark – the moon above the trees the prominent glow.

"You can't do this," I said, too angry to be scared. "You can't just take someone out of existence!"

The being lifted one of its wavering arms and gestured it toward the door. I looked to see James now there. He stopped, facing the door.

"Dan," he said, slightly turning to face me – *another me* – standing beside a parked RAV4, this time facing the door. "Who killed him?"

After a brief hesitation, the version of me beside the car answered him. Then, James grabbed the handle and went in. And so did we. Or, at least I did. I saw the candle on the small round table. Beside it, the red pencil. James approached it cautiously. Then he looked to me.

"Dan?" he asked. "How'd you get in here so fast?"

Surprised, I stepped toward him and gave him the utensil. "Don't worry about it," I said. "Just sign your name and make the wish."

He took it and wrote his name. He wrote it, not under the name *Melissa* like I thought he would. But beneath a different name which lay written beneath hers. A new name.

Allyster.

James, with his name fully marked, stood back up.

"I wish that Melissa didn't kill Allyster."

I looked at him, my head shaking. "Wait, no," I yelled. "Say..."

"Dan!"

"Say you wish he never died!"

"What are you talking about, dude?"

James looked at me. So did Eric, Mr. Crowley, and everyone else in the hall.

"James," I breathed as the light stung my eyes. "What did you wish for?"

"I don't know what you're talking about!"

"What's going on?" Mr. Glad pushed through the crowd, a concerned teacher by his side.

"Looks like we've got him back," Mr. Crowley said.

I looked around at everyone in disbelief. They looked at me like I was crazy. So did Mr. Glad. The same man who had told us that the force behind the door could be something called the djinn.

But he didn't.

It was what he would have told us after V came into the cafeteria.

Or would he have?

At that moment, Mike searched for a way to kill the djinn, or whatever it may be. He was somewhere north. *Alone.*

"Are you alright?" Eric asked.

I looked to him and to James as I nodded. "Yeah."

"Alright," Mr. Glad said to the other students. "Everyone can move along. Thanks for your concerns." He came up beside me. "Dan, I think we should call your parents and you should go home and rest."

I nodded, looking to my friends. "Sorry, guys."

• • • •

BOTH OF MY PARENTS were at work, so Mr. Glad had agreed to drive me. While in the silence of his car – him not wanting to pry on my episode, and me embarrassed – I gained up the courage to ask him something.

"Do you know anything about the door?"

"What door?" he asked, carefully.

"The one north of town."

He didn't say anything.

"The legend people are talking about," I clarified.

He arched his head back. "I don't think so," he said.

"Your daughters haven't gone looking for it?"

He looked at me strangely as he pulled into my driveway. "I don't have any daughters," he said.

I realized then that that was true. Mr. Glad had a son who currently attended my old elementary school. But no daughters.

"Oh," I said as I opened the door. "Sorry. Thanks for the ride."

"Get some rest," Mr. Glad said. "I know you have the play coming up this weekend, and surely a number of assignments. That mixed with the social life of a teenager... I understand it can be stressful, is what I mean," he said. "I'll tell them you won't be at practice tonight if you'd like. And we can discuss pushing some of your assignments when you come back."

"Okay," I said. "Thank you so much. That will help a lot."

He smiled as I got out and closed the door.

Once inside – the house to myself – I didn't want to play Warcraft like I would on any ordinary day I spent home from school. For, I couldn't concentrate on anything but the door. Too much strangeness had occurred.

Again, despite my fit in the hallway, everything seemed like it could be okay. Allyster was alive. James existed. Melissa liked me. She didn't want to kill Allyster. But V was out there, and he was about to come back with horrid news.

Right?

V had said there was no way to kill the being that granted the wishes. He said that it has always been here. But something about the time during which Allyster was dead seemed strange. And I had a theory about what had happened. The djinn must have known my plan to have someone wish Allyster's death away, so the being orchestrated those few days – with V and Mr. Glad – to make it sound like what we were up against held too much power for us to handle.

But what if it didn't?

Whatever the being may or may not have arranged for that time, I knew one thing for certain. V was out looking for help. *Somewhere far north.* I shouldn't have let him go it alone. But – with time not on my side, with the being manipulating me so easily, and with Allyster having made a wish – I had to find out as much of the truth as I could. And fast.

I picked up my phone and dialed V. As it rang, I sat down on my computer chair, worrying about what I may find out. Or what I may not find out.

He answered. At first, I heard no voice, only the sound of crunching. Perhaps snow. But it seemed far and booming.

"Hello?" Mike finally said.

"V," I said. "What have you found out? Things are getting intense and…"

"Dan!" he said, his voice muffled and crackling. The crunching seemed to be getting louder.

"V?" I said. "Where are you?"

"Look," he said, his faint voice in alarm. "You have to listen. I think he's here. You have to listen. I have a second before…"

Silence.

"V?"

Then just the crunching.

"Mike?" I shouted.

Then, quickly:

"I saw a shaman. The shaman told me that she knows what we're dealing with. It's a force that has been here a long time. You see, where it comes from, we can't go. That's why the door seems metaphysical. It's why going there is like a dream. We can go there, just not with our vessels."

"Vessels?"

"Our bodies. It grants wishes for us in our physical world in trade for people's souls so that when they die, they permanently go to wherever this thing lives. And it's not a good place. The shaman called it the underworld, but it sounds like hell."

"What do we do?" I panicked.

"We have to kill it."

"How?"

"You can't kill it," he said, his voice fading and frantic.

"V?"

"You have to trap it."

"What do you mean –"

"You have to trap it, Dan, and make sure it's somewhere it can never get out. It won't save us but it'll save others from... wait!"

"What's happening?"

"No, stop. You can't do –"

The line cut out. And Mike Veller's wish came true, for no one ever saw him again.

PART SIXTEEN

A s I stared at my phone's home screen in disbelief – having tried to call V back to no avail – a text popped up from Allyster:

Allyster> *Dude, I heard about what happened. Sorry I wasn't there. Are you alright?*

Allyster and I had only been friends for over a year, but once we became friends, we grew close. When it came to best friends, he was certainly in my top few. And as of recent, that was being diminished by a girl. We were both doing unspeakable things to try and beat the other out.

Or, at least I was.

I needed someone's help if I were to rid of this evil spirit, or whatever it may be. Out of all of my friends, Allyster was the most open to this stuff. And though I had already told Melissa most of the truth about everything, she only complicated things. Don't get me wrong, I still liked her. I still wanted to continue whatever was happening between us. But I had to finish this once and for all.

Dan> *I need your help with something important.*

Allyster> *Of course, buddy.*

Dan> *Your apartment tonight?*

Allyster> *Sure. What time?*

Dan> *Late.*

• • • •

MY PARENTS HAD GONE to sleep. Peeking down the hall, I saw their bedroom lamps turn out. Then, I waited another half-hour before I geared up for the cold.

In the spirit of getting this done quick and clean – no distractions and as small a risk as possible so that life could resume normally – I didn't want my parents to know that I was leaving. After the phone call they had received earlier from my principal, I figured that they wouldn't be eager to let me go "hang out" with my friends. So, the task had to be done in secret.

Night was best, anyhow.

Outside was cold, dark, and still. A thin layer of snow lay atop the sidewalks which ran through my neighbourhood, and despite my desire to be discreet, the frigid powder crunched beneath my foot with each step.

I had forgotten how eerie the town could feel at night. I underestimated how much creepier it would be on a night I was out to kill – *to trap* – some sort of ancient earth demon. One that hadn't hesitated displaying its ability to mess with my mind.

I took out my phone.

Dan> *Halfway there.*

He responded immediately.

Allyster> *Kk.*

I went back into my messages, went to my conversation with Melissa, and began to type. But, then I deleted it. She hadn't responded to my last text, which I sent to her before she went to rehearsal. It was her first rehearsal as lead and I wanted to encourage her. But, she never replied. And she hadn't sent me another message all night. This was not normal, seeing as we had been texting non-stop for a while.

Or was that all fake?

I wanted to blame Allyster. But, with a crucial task before me – to save others from the same fate I had befallen – I decided that the matter could wait.

I turned a corner onto a long stretch of sleeping houses. But that night, the street looked different than any other time I had taken it at night. That time, the road was terribly dark. All of the streetlights were out – not a single one illuminated. I could see – about twenty or so houses down – the street I would turn right onto afterward. The lights on that road were lit, the safety of them awaiting me.

I stood for a moment, took out my phone, then put it back into my pocket. Despite the cold, I began to sweat. I contemplated turning back, or taking a longer way.

"No," I whispered to the cold air. "Not this time."

I started down it, my heart pounding, my legs moving swiftly. I kept my eyes on the prize – the lit street at the end.

Of course, the lights could have been out for a number of reasons. Perhaps the block's power had simply gone out. Or there was ongoing maintenance.

Or it's him...

The thought shot through my head, seemingly from nowhere, pushing my legs faster. But they slowed when I heard a sound. Loud and from my left. The ring of a bell. As I turned and looked daringly, I saw a house with its lights on. Someone stood on the porch. But as I looked closely, I realized that it wasn't just someone. It was one of the hockey players from my school. One of the ones who would yell about the leprechauns after hearing me talk about the door. He rang the doorbell again, then turned to look at me. He wore an impossibly wide grin. His eyes briefly blazed into mine until he turned back, the door opening. Melissa answered, wearing her pajamas. Upon seeing him, her face tensed in fear. She stepped back with a cry.

"Please, no," her cry squawked into the night. He stepped toward her, then stopped. He turned to face me again, this time not so happy. His grin had been replaced with a snarl and his blazed eyes were now callous and black.

"What the hell are you looking at, asshole?"

He stepped – no, leapt – off of the porch, coming toward me. Behind him, Melissa watched intently. Her eyes were now black as well, her face no longer fearful, but indifferent.

"Nothing," I backed away.

But he didn't relent. He came toward me quicker. I turned and ran – hurrying as quickly as I could to the light at the end of the road. His footsteps pounded the pavement rapidly behind me, moving in quickly. I could hear his breath and the vulgar utterances of what he planned on doing to me once he got me.

With my chest ready to explode and my legs moving wildly – out of my control – I made it to the end of the street, turning onto the lit one. But my foot hit the smallest chunk of ice – likely something that had fallen off of a car – and I slid swiftly and painfully onto the salty road. I scrambled to fight off the jock, but his grasp never came. Breathing violently, I looked down the street I had just run down. It was empty – save for a few parked cars – and lit finely by a row of streetlamps.

• • • •

Dan> *Here.*

ALLYSTER LET ME UP, putting his finger to his lips as he opened the door. We crept up to his unit and not a word was said until we made it behind his apartment door with it shut and locked.

He walked over to the kitchen and grabbed a bag of chips as I took off my shoes.

"So, what's going on, man?" he asked.

"Alright, look," I rubbed my forehead. "It's about the door."

He nodded slowly as he bit down on a few chips.

"There's more to it than you might think," I said.

He nodded. "I know."

"You know what?"

"I know about your friend who went missing."

"How?"

He hesitated. "Melissa told me. We're talking again," he stared at me before quietly adding: "Just as friends, though."

"I'm glad you guys could make amends," I said, a little hurt that she had told him what I had confided in her about. "Well, my friend – V – he went to go find out anything he could about the door and the being who lived within it."

"Being?"

"I don't know how much you know. But I'm just going to fill you in now. And I don't care if you think I'm crazy, because it's all real. The door is metaphysical. You find it by strange means. Behind it – or around it – is this earth-demon type thing. Like a djinn."

"A djinn?"

"Just – it's like a demon – and it grants whoever goes through the door a wish in exchange for their soul."

"Wait, how do you know that?"

"V told me. He found out everything. It slowly comes for you. It screws up the wishes, probably to drive people closer to death so he can have their soul sooner."

"He?" Allyster's eyes seemed scared. Or worried.

I knew what he was thinking. The reality of his wish – the one he had made before James had made the wish to bring him back – was now clear to him. How or when Allyster went to the door, I didn't know. But the real question remained: what did he wish for? I, for some reason, couldn't ask him as I stood there in his kitchen. I wasn't sure I wanted to know. He was talking to Melissa again, and maybe their reconciliation had to do with his bidding behind the door.

"It," I shrugged. "I don't know. Whatever."

"Okay..."

"I need your help killing it."

"You came over here to ask me to help you kill a demon?"

"Yes," I said. "And, actually, we have to trap it."

"Trap it how?"

"I have a plan."

. . . .

"HOW DO YOU KNOW THIS is going to work?" Allyster asked as we walked farther into the park.

"It will if you let it," I told him.

There was a park a block away from Allyster's apartment. If you walked past the playground and through the soccer field, you would quickly find yourself in a trail through a wooded area by the lake. I figured – neither of us with a licence – it would be the best way to find the door, now that I knew of its true nature.

As we travelled deeper down the trail, we heard the lake's waves. The moon hid above the coniferous trees which towered over us with indifference. Quickly, it became too dark to see anything but their trunks.

"This is crazy," he breathed from behind me.

I stopped and turned, squinting to see his figure standing in the middle of the path. Thankfully, people walked their dogs through these woods during the day, patting down the snow. But some parts were icy and slippery. Also, it was cold. Allyster was right. This was a little crazy. What if it didn't work?

"This is probably good enough," I whispered.

"Okay," he looked around at the nothingness. "So, what do we do?"

"Well," I said to him, feeling braver in the dark, "you've been to the door before..."

"Yeah, and then Melissa started freaking out, so we left."

"Not that time," I replied coldly.

He stayed quiet.

"You went again," I said. "You made a wish."

"Okay," he said. "I did go again. I mean, I might have. I'm not sure."

"What do you mean?"

"I mean," he sighed. "I fell asleep last night instead of eating my pizza for some reason. But I dreamt that I went to the door. It was realer than real though. I don't know how I got there and I'm not sure how I got back. But... I was there."

I nodded, though I doubt he saw.

"And I did go through the door. I did make a wish. It was all so realistic. But... how did you know?"

"You signed your name."

He sighed again.

"What did you wish for?" I asked him. "Did it come true?"

"I don't know yet."

"What did you wish for?"

"Nothing."

"Tell me," I demanded.

"It's none of your business."

"It is," I stepped toward him. He was much stronger than me, but likely not as pissed. I knew the wish had to have something to do with Melissa talking to him and not me. "The wish is going to backfire," I said. "I need to help you control the blowback the best you can."

"There's no way it could backfire, okay?" he snapped. "I was clear about it."

"Doesn't matter."

He turned to walk off, but I grabbed his arm. "Tell me," I shouted.

"Okay," he yelled back. "Jesus. I wished for Melissa to hate you."

Within the blink of an eye, the moon grew strong, casting down into the forest. The pines vanished, replaced with bare deciduous trees. I could now see Allyster's face – one of worry and anger – and he could see mine. We weren't on the path anymore. We were on *a* path, but not the one by Allyster's apartment. The sound of the lake had vanished, replaced by the stillness which surrounded the door.

"How could you?" I said into the silence as he glanced around at our new setting.

"I'm sorry," he said. "I got desperate."

And, obviously, so had I.

"Let's just do this," I said, my stomach turning at the thought of what Melissa had done to Allyster when she'd been wished to hate him. The thoughts she'd had about him – thoughts she was now having about me.

How do I fix this one?

"How exactly do we do this?" Allyster asked.

"We get him on the other side of the door. Then we lock him in."

"How do we lock up a demon?"

I pulled my backpack around and zipped it open, taking out a hammer and a series of nails.

"The nails are iron. I did a bit of research today. Iron is considered a type of metal that wards off demons, including the djinn. We're going to nail the door shut. On the other side of it is his world. If we cut off that barrier, we should be able to stop him from coming back. At least I hope."

"How do we get him in there?"

"The same way he's been getting us in there," I started toward the door. "We trick him."

• • • •

I TRULY DEBATED OMITTING this next part, or at least lying about what had happened. I'm not proud of it. It's one of the things I think about almost nightly. For, we're all here now, and – in this moment, as I write this and you read it – he's somewhere else and the devil can only imagine what he is experiencing. However, I knew I had to include it. It is an integral part of the story, which has so far been truthful, and I won't stray from that honesty.

Anyone with influence doesn't believe me anyhow. Maybe you won't either. It's likely better that way.

Regardless, I'll fix it all soon.

The door opened, gliding on squeaky hinges into darkness. It was a darkness unlike that which we'd just experienced in the woods of the park. The moon's glow cast upon this curtain of black as though it were a wall. The matter of another world stood before us and our moon had no business illuminating it.

We had a plan. The door was now open and we both stood before it. I looked toward Allyster and nodded.

"Whatever you do," I whispered. "Don't let this door close until we see him in there and I'm back out here."

I began to walk in, but he stopped me.

"Wait," he said. "I'll do it."

"What?"

"I want to make a wish for real, anyway," he whispered, stepping past me. "To try and reverse what I've done."

I wasn't sure if you could make a wish with one still active, but I wasn't about to stop him from trying – especially if it meant Melissa wouldn't hate me.

"Okay," I nodded.

I held the hammer tight, a series of nails in my other hand at the ready. I pushed my body toward the open door, holding it there as I watched Allyster nearly vanish into the darkness. But then we both saw. He looked down at it – a small flickering candle on a slightly bigger table. Beside the chamberstick lay the red pencil.

He turned back to me. I nodded.

"I'm here to make a wish," he said, grabbing the pencil and writing his name beneath his previous signature.

In the distance – somewhere farther into that blackness – came another glow. One of fire.

The glow was him. It. Whatever.

"Now," I said sharply, yet quietly, to Allyster.

"Wait," he said, also looking at the glow. It grew, the figure of a person forming. Then, loudly, he announced: "I wish that Melissa loved me."

"What?" I shot.

He turned toward me. "Sorry, Dan."

With the djinn nearly at the candle, its grin nasty, I pulled the door shut. Despite Allyster's cries from the other side, I lined up a nail and began hammering it through the corner of the door and into the frame.

PART SEVENTEEN

It happened again, but different.

"Have you seen Allyster?" Eric asked.

I shook my head. I stood by my locker as other students passed hurriedly by, the world's ambience different now. The being was gone, but so was Allyster.

"Dude?" Eric squinted at me. "Are you having another panic attack?"

"What?" I said. "No. Sorry, dude. No, I don't know where Allyster is. He's probably sick."

James, who I hardly even noticed had been standing beside Eric, chimed in: "You know that guy would come to school even if he was dying."

"Yeah," I faked a chuckle.

"You're coming to rehearsal tonight, right?" Eric asked. "You need to practice with Melissa since she's the lead now. It's our last rehearsal before opening night."

"Right," I said. "Yeah, of course."

I had forgotten about rehearsal and the play in general. But I was glad to remember. It'd be a good chance for me to see and talk to Melissa. She'd yet to text me back, leaving me to worry that Allyster's original wish still influenced her.

"Well, off to class," James said.

"See you guys later," I mumbled as I turned and headed the opposite way.

So far, I'd had no indication that the djinn still stalked me. The previous night, I had sealed the door. And as I had driven the last nail into the wood, I moved to strike it once more – Allyster's cries bringing me to tears, blurring the scene – but instead of the nail, the hammer continued to move through the air. The tool slipped out of my hand and, with a splash, slipped into the waves of the dark lake. I had been standing on the edge, right where the earth dropped off a couple of metres into the water.

And I was alone.

The walk home – guilt and worry whirring around me – passed with no hallucinations of ill-intentioned jocks. And my dreams were haunted only by the idea that I had eternally trapped Allyster in a hellish realm.

Now, the entity made of smokeless fire didn't seem to exist. So far, the world around me felt different. Different in a normal way – the way it had felt before V had told me about the door. The world around me now felt plainly material.

One question remained, however. With the being and the door perhaps truly gone, could a previously made wish possibly still effect someone out here in the physical world?

· · · ·

MY NERVES WERE HIGH all day about rehearsal. Not because of the play. Not because I was rusty on my lines. But because I would see Melissa and, more likely than not, she would ask me where Allyster was and why he hadn't been replying to her texts. But, little did I know, he *had* replied to her texts. Or, at least one of them.

"Dan," Mrs. Dixie said as I entered the backstage area. Everyone turned to look. "Nice to finally have you. I hope you've been practicing your lines."

"As much as I can," I said. I started toward Eric, my eyes darting around for Melissa.

"Unfortunately," Mrs. Dixie continued, not to me or to anyone in particular. "Melissa won't be joining us."

"What?" I stopped and turned toward her.

"Yes," she nodded. "She said she had a family emergency. So, as I've done for you the last few times, I will stand in for her tonight the best I can."

"Dude," Eric came up to me. "Don't worry about it. This is the last rehearsal before opening night. You have to nail it. You've hardly run the last few scenes."

"I know," I slid my backpack off. "Just... Melissa and Allyster are both gone today."

"And?"

"I don't know," I said. "I've got to get into wardrobe."

· · · ·

"THE NUMBER YOU HAVE dialed is unavailable. Please hang up and try your call again."

Sitting in my room, rehearsal long over, I kept the phone to my ear. It was the third time I had tried. The recording repeated:

"The number you have dialed is unavailable. Please hang up and try your call again."

I hung up, but didn't try again. Melissa had refused to respond to my texts or answer my calls. I just needed to know if she was okay.

Or if she hated me.

Or if she loved him.

Him. Allyster. I had trapped him and I didn't have to. And somehow, I knew Melissa ghosting me had something to do with him. So, as I sat in my room, looking out at the cold landscape of my backyard and the conjoining lots, I knew. I had to go back to the door.

• • • •

IT WAS AFTER MIDNIGHT, frigid, and silent. I paced quickly to where we had found the door last time, another hammer in my bag. This time it would pry the nails it had formerly embedded. But first, there would be a stop.

Comparable to last night, the walk was uneventful. I travelled to Allyster's apartment without a glimpse of anything that could have been created by the being behind the door. Unless that thing waited for me outside of his building. Unless it was what I had happened upon in the eerie tranquility of my town's late hours: a Volvo.

Up above, Allyster's windows were illuminated. Before me, Melissa's car was parked. She was inside. She must have been. Allyster had turned off the lights when we had left last night. I looked up at them in wonder. Was she there because she loved him? Did his wish stick? Was *he* in there? Had he made it back?

The lights turned off. I took a deep breath. Maybe he was and they were together. As I stood on the sidewalk, my despondence accumulating, there came movement. It was through the main entrance and past the foyer. Legs came down the stairs. Melissa's legs.

In a panic, I jumped backward, out of her view in the nick of time. But that only bought me a second. I used it to scurry back farther, into the shadows of an alley.

I heard the door open, then close. Her footsteps marched toward her car. It had been facing away from me, so I peered out. It was indeed her, alone. Once in her car, she started it, then promptly drove off.

I pulled out my phone and found Allyster in my contacts. I called him. It went straight to voicemail. Back out on the sidewalk, I peered into the foyer. She had gotten inside, but how, if not by Allyster?

I began walking toward the park. As I did, I decided to text Melissa something she could not ignore.

Dan> *So? Was Allyster home?*

I nonchalantly slid my phone back into my pants pocket like I didn't just send a bombshell of a text. I continued into the park, then across it. The trees soon enveloped me, hiding me from Melissa were she to double back. And maybe she did, maybe she didn't. But, finally, my phone vibrated.

I stopped and took a breath. I stood on the same path Allyster and I had been walking down last night. The same path I had taken back alone last night. I pulled out my phone. The text would decide on whether I head back home or search for the door.

Melissa> *No. What did you do to him?*

Dan> *Oh, so you can text.*

Melissa> *Yeah, and I was texting Allyster last night. He said he was going out with you at 1 a.m.*

I looked up into the darkness, a little worried. A blob floated ahead of me, the light of my phone having blinded me. I put it back into my pocket, hoping that once my eyes adjusted, the door would appear and I wouldn't have to answer to that text. But the door never materialized. Not that night. Not any night.

• • • •

I WALKED THE WOODS for hours. I would stop and wait, closing my eyes and hoping for the door to appear once I opened them. But it never did. There was not a whisper or a sound to indicate that the door still existed.

Melissa's text had been pretty damning, and I never replied. Thankfully, she skipped school the next day. I prepared to deny Allyster's text to her up and down, saying that he must have made it up. But she wasn't there to grill me. Though, I kept worrying she would be. I became increasingly nervous that she would show up and, in front of everyone, blame me for Allyster's disappearance.

See, at first I thought I could deny things. But during third period an announcement was made. Just like before, except now it was real. There were no take-backs this time. Not if I couldn't find the door. Allyster was considered a missing person once again.

I write now about what really happened, but it will never be believed. You all now know where he truly went. Whether you believe it or not, at least you have the truth before you.

I was supposed to go to work that night, but I called in sick. I couldn't risk Melissa coming to interrogate me about Allyster's text. Not after the announcement. As soon as it was made, my heart sunk. Everyone was concerned and worried because of something I'd done. And though I had hoped to keep that aspect to myself, Melissa had other plans.

• • • •

IT WAS SATURDAY NIGHT. Opening night. I still hadn't spoken with Melissa. But – along with a full house, everyone's family in the audience – she came. As the backstage crew ran around making preparations, as the cast got into costume, make-up, and microphoned, I tried to steal a moment to go talk to her. I wanted to tell her – to lie to her – that I had no part in Allyster's disappearance and that the text was likely a cover for him going somewhere else. I wanted to offer to help her search for him. I wanted to be on her side, even if it was predicated on a lie – one that I would take to the grave if I had to.

Unfortunately, through the madness, I never got a chance to speak to her. I had to say a number of things to her that night, all of which a playwright scripted long ago. I was supposed to *kiss* her. Before, I had built it up in my mind as an exciting moment. But after everything, I dreaded it. And either way, the kiss never happened.

Maybe it would have been different if I'd been able to talk to her first.

• • • •

MELISSA WAS A GREAT actor. Despite my own qualms during the first two acts, she performed stunningly, as though she didn't suspect me of killing her friend. But that acting crumbled to ashes come the kiss. At the end of the third act, with just a few moments to go before I could set things straight with her behind the curtain, she stopped. We stood face to face. Alone on the stage, all the eyes in the darkness of the crowd were on us. It was the moment in which we were supposed to embrace one another as lovers together at last. I leaned in and so did she. But instead of a kiss, she whispered:

"I'm going to destroy you."

Her microphone picked up her words, whether everyone had heard exactly what she'd said or not. But it didn't matter, for there was more.

Melissa stepped back and faced the crowd. "Allyster is missing because of Dan," she announced. "Allyster texted me at 1 a.m. the night he went missing saying that he was going out with Dan." She pulled out her phone and faced it toward the audience, as though they'd be able to see.

"What are you doing?" I shot.

The crowd and the actors offstage, along with Mrs. Dixie, were all too stunned to interrupt.

"I'm exposing you."

"I didn't do anything," I went into my prepared defence. "He must have been using that as an excuse to go do something else."

She looked back down at her phone. "Then why did he send me *this* text two hours later?"

"Two hours?" I squinted at her phone.

And indeed, there was another text. Coming before a series of panicked, unanswered texts from Melissa – some of which had her professing her love to him – Allyster had sent a message from the other side.

Allyster> *Help! He trapped me behind the door.*

PART EIGHTEEN

The morning was bright. The blue sky and the sun among it shone sharply down onto a fresh layer of snow from the previous night. From Saturday night. From the night Melissa had *exposed* me.

She'd done one hell of a job.

The door, gone or not, works mysteriously. After all of the time since the event, and all of the research I've been able to do, the only conclusion I can come up with is that you can shut one door, but you can't shut them all. For, as the morning sun shone intensely across our town, a dog-walker stumbled across the body of a missing teenager.

• • • •

"WE NEED TO TALK ABOUT this in private," I had told Melissa on the auditorium stage.

My voice boomed through the speakers placed around the audience. Their stares were wide, mouths agape – getting much more than their admission tickets were worth.

"There's nothing you have to say to me that you can't say in front of everyone."

"But you know everything," I told her. "They don't. You'll understand. *They won't.*"

"What do I know?"

"You know about the door. About V..."

"You mean your friend that no one else has seen before?"

"What?" I spat. "He came into the school and yelled at me in front of everyone."

She frowned. "What are you talking about?"

"Oh yeah," I mumbled. "That was before," I explained. "I'd made a bad wish and had to reverse it. But it had brought us closer together. We kissed. For real. We *had sex.*"

She stepped back, aghast. "Are you insane?"

"No," I said. "Fine. Look, Allyster made a bad wish. We had gone to close the door for good, and he had made a bad wish," I looked to the crowd, trying to get them on my side. But they were just as appalled as Melissa. I had to hide the truth. Just a bit of it. "It took him away. He just... vanished with the door."

"I'm going to kill you like you killed him," she shrieked.

Melissa jumped on me. I fell hard on the floor, hurting my tailbone. She went for my neck, but it wasn't long-lived. There was quickly a dozen people pulling her off of me. Someone had apparently called the police – likely at the first accusation of my involvement with Allyster's disappearance – because at some point amidst the blur of everything, there were police officers present.

Melissa and I were separated and questioned. I fight to remember this night, as it's a horrendous haze within my mind. Though, I can recall a few certain images. The officers had pressed me on the whereabouts of Allyster. Despite my earlier admission to Melissa – and to hundreds of other people – about being with Allyster that night, I stuck to my story that he had made up the text. That I had no part in any of it.

Only two other things stand out in my mind: the look on Eric and James' faces as I was being questioned, and the faint glimmer of an illuminated humanoid entity outside of the theatre's windows, gazing in at it all.

• • • •

WITH NO OTHER EVIDENCE besides a text which was somewhat open to interpretation, I was able to go home that night. I left with my angry, confused, and upset parents, along with a cruiser which followed us to our house, indicating that they suspected me more than I had hoped.

It was clear which camp my family had chosen. They thought I was crazy. When we got inside, I tried to plead my case to them – the same bit I had told the officers – but they wanted none of it. They simply told me to go to my room. So, I did. And though the thought of escaping and trying to find the door once more to bring Allyster home flooded my mind, I didn't act on it. I knew it would be futile. If the djinn was behind this, it certainly wouldn't let me find the door and return Allyster. If it wasn't, I suspected that the cruiser which had followed us home now stood guard on our street somewhere.

Like I had said before, a mere twelve hours later somebody found and reported Allyster's body. He – if it was ever truly him and not a decoy of some sort created by the djinn – had washed up from the lake, onto the rocks. By the time that the body had been recovered, autopsied, and a conclusion had been made, it wasn't even sundown. The police were knocking on our door with a search warrant.

Strangely, I felt nothing as I stood halfway up our stairway, looking down on the door as my father opened it to the police and they announced their purpose. My mom sauntered over to the door, glancing up at me.

"Dan, we're going to search your bedroom," one of the officers said as my parents let them in.

I nodded, the most movement I was able to make. They both walked past me, up the stairs.

"Turn right down the hall," my mother's voice echoed around me. "First door on the left."

I stood there for thirty-seconds or an hour. The officers returned. One of them gripped my arm and I felt handcuffs going around my wrists.

"Daniel, I am arresting you for suspected murder," he said. "You have the right to retain and instruct counsel without delay. You also have the right to free and immediate legal advice from duty counsel. Do you understand?"

"Yes," I mumbled with tears in my eyes.

"Do you wish to call a lawyer?"

"Yes," I said, the sobs of my mother louder than the officer's words.

"You also have the right to apply for legal assistance through the provincial legal aid program. Do you understand?"

"Yes."

As the other officer passed me, I saw in his hand a large Ziploc bag containing the second hammer I had taken from my dad's toolbox.

• • • •

ERIC, NOR JAMES, EVER came to visit me. I haven't seen them once in all these years. I also haven't seen Melissa. My parents, who succumbed to the notion that I was mentally ill, stopped visiting after the first year.

I was tried for murder. In court, I testified, sharing the truth of that night to the best of my ability. I explained the door and what it did. I explained the wish Allyster had made regarding Melissa and what that meant. And I told them that I had locked him behind the door even though there was likely time for him to run out. Despite all of this, the prosecutor revealed to the judge and jury – and myself – that the fake Allyster had been bludgeoned to death with a tool fitting the one they had found in my backpack: a hammer. A witness testified to seeing me walking into the woods near where Allyster's body was found the night after his death. That, along with the texts, convinced everyone.

They reasoned that I had sent the second text to Melissa before I discarded his phone in one way or another. My lawyer pleaded insanity on my part, but it was denied, the judge stating that I likely decided to spin a tale to get a lesser sentence.

However, they did seem to be in a general agreement that I was not mentally stable. For, I stuck to my story, and despite all of the truths that had happened over those few months, nobody believed me. Or, what's more likely, is that they didn't want to. Mike Veller was gone once again, and though no evidence showed my involvement with that, people suspected it.

They wouldn't listen when I told them that his disappearance was due to the djinn.

I was seventeen when I was found guilty of first-degree murder. Under the *Youth Criminal Justice Act* in my country, as a minor, my maximum sentence can only be ten years. And that's what it was, along with regular psychiatric evaluations.

However, the djinn is still out there. It has my soul, Melissa's soul, James' soul, Allyster's soul, and who knows who else's soul. When I die, my spirit will depart, but not to go where any other soul goes. It will go to him, in his world. It will be gone from this universe forever.

Unless I can get it back.

The inspiration to write this story came when I received a letter a few years ago. At my family's request, my trial was largely unpublicized, but somehow she had heard my story. From the far north of my country – beyond where the roads go – the shaman claimed to know how to find my friends. She was the last person to see V alive and the only person who believes my side of the story.

My sentence began in the summer of 2010 and it ends in the summer of 2020. When I get out, I'll prove to everyone my innocence. First, with this story, and second, by revealing what is in Allyster's casket.

I left Allyster behind the door, in another world. His "body" was a fabrication created by the entity behind the door in order to frame me. His death was a lie to trap me where I couldn't get to the door any longer.

Finally, I'll prove myself by finding the real Allyster. I'll bring him back. I'll fix what I've made wrong. I'll do what V couldn't and find a way in, defeat the monster, and bring my two friends back.

You can close one door, but you can't close them all. There are others out there. Other entryways to these worlds.

Have you, dear reader, seen one of these doors in the forest, the desert, or anywhere else a door ought not be? If so, *do not* enter it. But please, do tell me its location, so that I can.

Whether you believe the narrator's tale or not, thank you for taking the time to read it.

• • • •

IF YOU ENJOYED THE story, please leave a review. It helps more than you may think.

• • • •

TO BE ALERTED ABOUT new releases of stories like this one, go to www.highstrangeness.ca[1], scroll to the bottom of the page, and subscribe to the High Strangeness newsletter. **You will only be e-mailed when there is a new release.**

---

1. http://www.highstrangeness.ca